Just Play Dead

St. Martin's Press New York

Just Play Dead

Dan Gordon

Design by Nancy Resnick

Library of Congress Cataloging-in-Publication Data

Gordon, Dan (Daniel).
    Just play dead / Dan Gordon.
      p. cm.
    ISBN 0-312-16876-4
    I. Title.
    PS3557.065455J87   1997
    813´.54—dc21   97-14779 CIP

First Edition: October 1997

10 9 8 7 6 5 4 3 2 1

For Linda,
who fills my heart with ecstasy,
my days with light,
and my life with love

Acknowledgments

This book was written at a particularly difficult time, full of the kind of life changes that can destroy years of discipline. In this instance, the writing of the book itself, while cathartic for me, was I am sure, a giant pain in the ass for others. For Lenore Lewis, who put up with a madman for the months of the writing of this book and the trauma that preceded and followed it, as always my undying gratitude. I think that no one outside of myself, better loves or understands Jack Wolfe than Mrs. Lewis. Her wit and taste were the constant acid test for this piece of work. As always, my thanks go to Jerry Zeitman, whose constant encouragement and faith in this project and in me have been one of the happiest things in my life. To Shawn Coyne, who began the process in the earliest conversations and to Dana Edwin Isaacson, who continued the process of editing this book, my deepest appreciation. No writer could ever ask for more support from any editors. Indeed, the entire experience at St. Martin's Press has been a total joy from the start, and continues to be. To Melanie Griffith, Diane Sillan, Christine Peters, and Harold Becker, who have championed this work tirelessly, my deepest and heartfelt thanks. No one could ask for better partners on any project. To the folks at the Four Seasons Hotel in Maui who were so kind in enabling me to find and research the locations used in this book, Mahalo, t'anks, eh bra? To the many men and women engaged in law enforcement in Maui, in particular Captain Tam Ho and Officer Loren Ellias of the Lahaina Patrol, Maui Police Department, and Captain Gerald Matsunaga of the Wailuku Patrol, Maui Police Department, who were so kind with their time and expertise. I would particularly hope that the reader would stop and bow his head for a moment in memory of Sister Roberta Derby, founding Chaplain of the Honolulu Police Department, whose company and counsel were both an inspiration and a joy. To Skipper Rick Kleine and his First Mate, Mike Estes of the "Flexible Flyer," my gratitude for showing me how to blow up a boat and make it look like an accident. To my sons, Zaki, Yoni, and

Adam, as always my thanks for being the best sounding boards and friends any father could have. And finally, again, to Linda, who listens to my stories.

Just Play Dead

One

It started with the woman. Yeah, I guess you could say that it started when she got the itch. I mean if you're looking for that moment when things perhaps took a turn down a road that led one way to somebody being killed, then perhaps that's as good a point to pick as any. Maybe given who she was, and who she was married to, and who she would meet, and who would see it happen, from that point on everyone's fate was sealed; who would live and who would die, who would kill and who would be killed, who by fire and who by drowning, who would wander and who would be tranquil, who would be betrayed . . . well everyone would be betrayed.

No one would be faithful, except God maybe.

God would come out all right on this one. God would come out just fine. He doesn't always, but on this one he would.

Ah, a murder mystery with a Semitic twist. A Haimishe little murder, a little Yiddish film noir perhaps? Woody Allen and a shiksa doing detective shtick in the Big Apple, talking trash at Elaine's about whether Mr. Feinberg offed his wife to run off with his secretary? No, not this time. This was in Maui and the only Jew in the story was me and I'm not in the story. I just know the story. Knew the woman too, once even in the biblical sense. Maybe I was a candidate for the job the boy toy eventually got.

Maybe she was looking even then for someone who would be so . . . what's the word in the cologne ad . . . obsessed? Someone who would be so obsessed with her, so crazy for the taste and touch and smell of her, someone who wanted her so much he felt like a drowning man and she was air. Drowning men can kill you. They do that for air. And who better than a cop, who knew how to cover his tracks, who knew just what the investigators would be looking for and how to give them what they wanted and lead them away from you, who better than a cop to kill your husband? Maybe I would have done it too, if she had chosen me instead of the boy. Wait. Hold on. That was too jarring, wasn't it? Here I was talking about a sexy little hit, a ménage à murder and then I said something about a Jewish cop in Maui? Not only that but a Kosher-keeping scuba-diving cowboy Jew who's a conservative Republican and a former sergeant in the Israeli Army–type Jewish cop in Maui. Trust me. Nothing's what it seems in paradise. You think you've been there? You were a tourist. You haven't got a clue.

Case in point. Rich lady gets bit in half by a shark. Haole like me gets sent down to take the report. Rich Haole lady, you got to have a report for the Haole insurance company on the mainland. The Major, as in my boss, says mo' betta the Haole insurance company see a Haole name on the bottom of the report. That way they don't think it's one of us buggahs goin' cockroach da kine. No talk stink.

Lest you think the Major is a graduate of the Ponce Ponce School of Advanced English Studies, let it be pointed out that he has a master's from Berkeley. The Major simply likes to give me shit. That is because my name is Kahana. Denil Kahana, though everybody calls me Dani. Now the Major is what the locals call a Chang, as in a Hawaiian of Chinese decent, though that term can also be used to connote cheapness, a Chang being even tighter than a Pak'e, another word for a Chinese Hawaiian. At any rate, locals like to give Haoles shit. Plenty good fun, eh bra? I got to Honolulu by way of LA, Tel Aviv, and LA again, and started working patrol for Honolulu P.D., where I was hot to make detective. I tried telling the Major back in Honolulu that there was probably some

Federal grant they could get for advancing a Jew to detective, that it would indicate racial diversity in a place where promoting an Asian or native Hawaiian gets no points with the Feds at all. The argument did not go over well. Then, as luck would have it, I saved the life of H.P.D.'s chaplain, a seventy-year-old nun named Sister Rachel, who I called Shvester Rochelle.

It seems some jarhead Marine captain is holed up with his wife and kid and says he's going to commit suicide after he offs the wife and kid because he caught the wife shtupping a nineteen-year-old black private first class, or maybe he was a lance corporal and had a first class set of privates . . . or lance for that matter.

At any rate Captain Jarhead is the last unreconstructed redneck asshole in Oahu and since the black kid wisely jumped out the window and Captain Jarhead has to kill somebody to relieve his tension, the wife and kid are it. Only thing is, Captain Jarhead is evidently a lapsed Catholic, who, since he is about to commit suicide wants to see a priest and be absolved before his impending murder/suicide. This is the kind of person who gives goyim a bad name.

Now the uniformed cop on the scene is the poster boy for Glens. Glens are nerdy Hawaiians of Japanese descent. They have shirt protectors in their pockets and their parents named all of them Glen. Glen Tanaka, Glenn Yamashita, Glen Nomo. Those are three Japanese Glens I know and I'm not even trying. So Officer Glen, trying to stall for time, tells Captain Jarhead that while the department doesn't have any priests on call, they do have a nun, Shvester Rochelle, or Sister Rachel, or Sister One, which is her radio call sign. At the same time Officer Glen is on the horn calling out a nine-ninety-seven officer-needs-help, the dispatcher calls for any unit in the vicinity *and* for Sister One. By the time I get there Sister One is a hostage with a nine-millimeter Baretta pointed at her head.

"Sister," I later say, "Does the phrase Goyisher kop have any meaning to you at all?"

Turns out Sister One goes into Captain Jarhead's house and offers herself up as a hostage, telling him that a departmental nun is worth more than a wife and kid any day of the week. Also, because of her advanced years she will be infinitely easier to handle. She lays a lot of Pat O'Brien You're-not-a-bad-boy-Butch shit on him and finally Jarhead agrees to let the kid go free. But now he's got the wife *and* the nun.

By this time the Major is reaming everyone a new sphincter for allowing our nun to get snatched. It is at this point in time that I see a chance to make detective since the Blue Nun is one of our chief's favorites. I change into a pair of Dockers and a luau shirt and grab the EMT's medicine bag and call Captain Jarhead, introducing myself as Doctor Kahana, Shvester Rochelle's internist. Sister One, who is a very sneaky old broad in her own right, picks up on the scam and starts complaining about chest pains while I tell Jarhead that a dead hostage is going to be no use to him at all. How does he know this isn't a trick and I'm not a cop?

"I'm a Jew," I say. "Have you ever heard of a Jewish cop in Honolulu for Christ's fucking sake?"

The notion that a Jew could never be a cop in Honolulu makes sense to this cracker asshole. However, he wants to know how he can be sure that I'm a *real* Jew.

I ask if he wants to hear my Haftora.

No response there.

I offer to show him my autographed Bar Mitzvah copy of the Protocols of the Elders of Zion signed by Henry Kissinger himself.

No cigar there either. I offer Woody Allen movie trivia and a list of the combo sandwiches at the Carnegie Deli using the comedians' names. The Shecky Greene . . .

Still no takers.

"My name is Kahana, you Jew-hatin' son of a bitch. You ever hear of Meir Kahana? He was my uncle. I'll send in my driver's license."

A goy hot mazel as we say in Hawaiian. The guy goes for it. I send in the license, Denil Kahana, bigger'n shit.

"All right Jew boy, come on in."

I come in and begin listening to Shvester's heart. That's when I ask her if the words goyisher kop have no meaning to her at all. At about this time Captain Shit-for-Brains (as I had now begun to think of him) asks Sister One if she really believes in Jesus. I could see this one coming a mile away and was about to suggest that Shvester take the Fifth or consider conversion, but she tells the guy, yeah, of course she believes in Jesus.

"Well," says Captain S.F.B., "Then you ought to thank me because you're going to meet him in about ten seconds. We all are," he says.

"Hey," I say. "I *don't* believe in Jesus."

"Fuck you, Yid," is the reply.

I look at Shvester and Shvester looks at me.

"Can I at least have a chance to pray?" she asks.

Jarhead says she can.

"What about me?" I ask. "I'd like a chance to davenen mincheh."

"What's that mean?" asks the cracker.

"It means I'd like to pray the afternoon prayers."

"It's nighttime," he says.

"It's all right," I say, "I'm in no hurry."

By this time however, I had managed to close a little distance with this cretin, just enough so that a swing of the EMT bag would connect with the Baretta, and then I go flying up onto him, grab his gun hand, and the two of us go up and back over the sofa behind him. When we come up, I've got his hand wristlocked behind him but he still hasn't dropped the Baretta and worse, he's starting to squeeze off rounds in the direction of my scrotum. It was then that I shouted out the words that proved to be my salvation.

"Sister Rachel, for the love of God, kick this cocksucker in the nuts!"

She looked like Jan Steneroude trying for three points from the fifty-yard line. She came straight up with those big old nasty nun shoes with the steel safety toes, launching Captain Shit-for-Brains into a profound out-of-body experience. He dropped the Baretta and I stuck my little mace spritzer (which I had secreted in the back pocket of the Dockers), halfway down his throat and emptied it in his bronchial passages. Then we turned him over to Sergeant Faleomavaega, a seven-foot-tall, three-hundred-and-seventy-pound Samoan who loved Sister One. The subsequent report said that the suspect, in a fit of suicidal despondency, broke free from Sergeant Faleomavaega and threw himself down the stairs. It did not matter that the building in question was only one story and its stair unit consisted of three steps. Law enforcement in paradise has certain advantages. Especially when the perp is a Haole and has no relatives of any importance on the island.

"Shvester," I said to the Blue Nun, "let's go get shitfaced."

"You're on," said Sister One.

There were no detective slots open at H.P.D. but the chief, in gratitude to me for having saved Sister Rachel's life and because he wanted me the hell out of his department, pulled some strings, called in some markers, and got me transferred to Maui County P.D. and upped to detective grade.

Unfortunately, saving nuns in Honolulu bought me precious few points in Maui. The Major did not like the fact that he just got stuck with a Haole cop who was promoted over the heads of the locals. That's when I made the mistake of telling the Major that I was not Haole, that I was in fact of Hawaiian descent and that my family's name was not Kahana but Ka*hu*na, and that they changed it to avoid anti–Pacific Rim prejudice when they moved to the mainland.

"They changed the name from a Hawaiian one to a Jewish one in order to avoid prejudice?"

"My parents were schmucks, is that my fault?" I asked.

From that day on, the Major liked to give me shit. He delighted in talking pidgin to me and I took to replying to him in Yiddish or Hebrew. So when the rich lady got bit in two by the shark, I was the one who got sent to do the report.

It happened just off Wailea Point near the big estates.

"What happened?" I asked the uniform.

"Rich Haole lady got bit by a shark," said the uniform. "Got bit in half."

"Bummahs," said I.

Bummahs, pronounced Bum-ahz, is an expression of regret. It seemed the only thing to say in the face of what was to me such an obvious-seeming accident. But remember what I said. Nothing's what it seems in paradise.

Joan Chan was the senior detective on that

case. She was thirty-four or thirty-five, with the kind of raven black long hair that you see in coconut oil shampoo commercials with the gorgeous Hawaiian girl in the lava lava kneeling on a rock in front of a waterfall-splashed lagoon, combing her hair with a sea comb and looking like every boy's wet dream of Bali Hai. That was Joan Chan at a glance.

That body, the dewy soft brown skin, the long black hair that cascaded over slender shoulders and that first look of Pacific innocence that made you think she might burst into a chorus of "Happy Talkie Talkin' Happy Talk," that made you pray she liked white guys, that was in your heart of hearts one of the reasons you came here in the first place . . . the siren's song that said gentle breezes and a beautiful Polynesian girl who didn't know from Neiman Marcus was waiting on your special island.

Kop Shmop.

Whoever dreamt up that illusion did not know Hong Kong girls in general or Joan Chan in particular. Joan Chan was from the *Wayne's World* Chinese Rock 'n' Roller Killer Babe School of Oriental Beauties. She was so cynical she made M. Butterfly look like a pussy. She was a black belt in kung fu.

She could do, and did, five hundred stomach crunches . . . every morning. The steel was not just in her abs, either. It was in her eyes. Story was that her grandfather, who was her only real family, came over from Hong Kong right after the war, settled in Maui, and then somewhere along the line after Joan's parents had died and the old man took her in, ran afoul of some sort of local gangster and lost his money or something. Joan became a cop with one ambition. To bust the guy who had ruined Grandpa. When the bad guy turned up very dead, there were rumors that Joan might have had something to do with it, but since the bad guy wound up quite literally as shark bait, there weren't enough clues to make a case against anyone but the shark.

Joan had a lot of ambition. She planned to stay in the department for another two years and then go into politics. That's where the real power was on the island, and the real money, and Joan wanted and understood both.

I was the first Jew she had ever met and I thought that might win me some points but she just said that if I was one of the smart ones I'd be a lawyer, not a cop. Needless to say, I never got on base with Detective Chan. Nor did anyone else as far as I knew. There were intimations she had a sugar daddy somewhere. But I wasn't buying it. She was all business, and copwise you couldn't ask for anyone better to be partnered with, especially on a case where the perp was a shark.

"You think it was an accident," she said, looking at me the way I used to look at guys who put mayo on pastrami.

"Well in the sense that it was an accident for

the rich Haole lady," I said. "I mean if the shark gets a good lawyer, we could probably never prove intent."

She asked me if I knew what kapu was. I'd heard the term in the luau shows more than any-place else. It was the cornerstone of the Hawaiian native religion as far as I understood it. There was kapu on this and kapu on that, meaning certain things were off limits to all but the royalty. Kapu was a way of defining those things which were pro-hibited or forbidden, an island way of saying traif.

"Kapu is also a way o' puttin' a curse on some-one," Joan said. "You got a beef with somebody, you got love troubles, somebody talking bad about you, doin' something evil, you can get a Kahuna or a priest, especially if it's somebody doin' somethin' bad to the whole community. You can get the Kahuna to put a kapu on that person. Word was," Joan explained, "that the rich Haole lady was a royal pain in the ass bitch. She had a young hus-band and plenty attitude. Her place was between the road and the water and a stretch of beach where the Hawaiians always went fishing, where they liked to go for religious celebrations. The Haole lady denied them access. Said anybody who cut across her land would be prosecuted for tres-passing. People tried to tell her this was minors, you know, no big t'ing. Nobody wants nothin' from her, just let them go down to the beach. Rich Haole lady wouldn't listen. No shame, plenty talk but. (In pidgin, the locals like to put the word *but* at the end of the sentence.) So the talk was somebody went to a Kahuna to put a kapu on the rich Haole lady."

"Like what kind of kapu?"

"The rich Haole lady goes for a swim every morning at nine o'clock. Everybody knows it. Everybody sees her every morning, nine o'clock, off Wailea Point. So the local gossip has it that somebody went to a Kahuna and the Kahuna did his kapu thing."

"Meaning what?"

"Meaning," said Joan, "that he called up the sharks, the amakua to come up from their caves where they sleep and eat the rich Haole woman."

"You believe that?" I asked.

"You don't?"

"No."

"Doesn't your Bible say that God called up a big fish to swallow Jonah?" she asked, and her look was what could only be described as inscrutable.

"That's what it says," I replied.

"So," said Joan Chan, "you think Jewish magic is more potent than Hawaiian magic?"

"I think the only reason God got caught in the first place was that Jonah ratted him out, and that Johnny Cochran could have got him off."

"I'll tell you what I think," she said.

She wasn't looking at me anymore. She was looking off past the tide pools and the breakers, out across the pristine water above the seven caves where the sharks sleep in the morning and where the rich Haole woman got bit through the midsection, neatly cutting her in two. But it wasn't scenery she saw and she was looking deeper than that forty or so feet to bottom depth. She looked like a fisherman who knows the waters well and knows that for whatever reasons, nothing will be caught today.

"Here's what I think," said Joan Chan. "I think her grieving young husband is going to turn up married to a nice local island girl. I think he's going to remove the kapu and let the locals cross his property down to the beach all they want. I think he's going to come into a lot of insurance money and spread it around and become very well liked. I think he was an experienced diver and he probably heard about the kapu talk and chummed the waters where his wife swam, chummed it with nice red meat dripping blood, then got himself out with that underwater scooter over there."

She pointed over to the yellow super-souped up James Bond scooter.

"I think it was the smell of the meat that called the sharks up and when his wife got there they were waiting. They were hungry . . . in a blood lust. They had started feeding and the meat ran out before their appetites did and if she hadn't shown up when she did, they probably would have taken to eating each other. They're sharks after all. I think that young husband knows a lot about sharks."

So did Joan Chan; enough to know there would be no way to prove anything that she'd said. She also knew a lot about politics and that Maui County would not want the matter pursued. Tourists are willing to accept the occasional shark attack into their vision of paradise, especially if it comes along with a little local lore about kapu-cursing Kahunas exacting revenge from local Leona Helmsley types. But murder is something else again. They don't talk about murder at the luau shows.

I wrote the report and signed my Haole name to it and the Haole insurance company on the mainland paid off and everyone was invited to the husband's wedding on the beach.

She was a local girl. Everybody had plenty good fun. There was plenty of beer in tubs full of ice and drinks with rum and a machine that dispensed killer frozen mai tais. There was a luau pig and sushi, plates of grilled ahi with teriyaki sauce and baked ono almondine and to cater to the locals, there was plenty of poi, my boy. I stood over by the side with Joan Chan watching the bride and groom dance as an Elvis impersonator flown in from Vegas sang the Hawaiian wedding song. Hawaiians love Vegas. Anyway, I was standing next to Joan Chan hoping that maybe she'd get tanked on mai tais and do something she'd regret and I would agree never to mention again, but all she did was sip at a Diet Pepsi while I got shit-faced.

"So," I slurred, "when do you think he got the idea?"

"Who?" she asked as her glance played across the veranda of the dead rich Haole lady's estate.

I could see her silently making calculations; how much for the land, the house, the furnishings and paintings. I knew that look. There were a few pawn brokers in my family, a jeweler or two. You could almost hear the abacus beads clicking.

"Prince Charming," I said trying not to drool mai tai from my numbing lips. "The happy groom and grieving widower?" I tried again.

"I don't know what you're talking about," said Detective Chan.

"Gai cock in hittel."

I finally got her to raise an eyebrow.

"What's that mean?" she asked.

"It means go shit in your hat, De*f*ective."

"I like that," replied my immediate superior. "It's almost Chinese."

"So when do you think he got the idea to turn his wife into shark bait?" I asked again. "When he heard that the locals were revving up their kapu curse or what?"

"Him?" she said, and her eyes flicked from the real estate back to the bronzed groom whose linen shirt was open now all the way down the front so you could see well-defined pecs as he dirty-danced his bride across the floor.

The bride worked as a lead dancer at the Sheraton, and the year before rumor had her linked to a movie star, not that she broke up his marriage. The wife just called her the last straw. But there was nothing strawlike about her, it's just that the movie star was tougher than anything or anyone they had on the islands. Beneath his famous smile and twinkling eyes, he was tougher than any of the sharks who had recently dined on the rich Haole lady. The bride was evidently drawn to men like that. There was something in fact about the groom that was reminiscent of the movie star.

"He's a shark," Joan Chan said of the groom.

"So when you think he got the idea to off his wife for the insurance?"

Joan looked at me with the coldest brown eyes of anyone I had ever seen since Golda Meir.

"That one? I think he got the idea the minute he laid eyes on her."

By now of course it should be obvious even to the casual observer that no one could possibly have more respect, not to mention admiration for Detective Joan Chan's obvious assets, judgment, and charms but when it comes to the exact moment of the sealing of one's fate, I think she has to take a back seat to the Jews.

We do this stuff every year. We know when the book is open and who's checking it twice and we know that when you hear that lonesome shofar blow, it ain't a Johnny Cash song, Jack, and it's not a factory whistle either. It's the big game buzzer in the sky. The book is closed, the refrigerator door is shut, the light is off, and the cheese is getting hard.

Yo' time is up. Yo' fate has been sealed. Trust me on that one. I been there.

October 6th. Yom Kippur, 1973, kickin' back at the kibbutz when I lived in Israel, where Yom Kippur is still as death, no radio, no TV, no cars on the roads, no children playing nor dogs barking when all the earth it seems holds its breath waiting, hoping, praying, one more day, one more month, good health, no death, not for me nor the ones I love, nor the ones who love me. If not for our sakes then for those of martyred fathers, sainted mothers, anyone who can buy us out of this thing between us and God, holding our breaths till sundown, till stars shine, till the fast is over, till the terror is gone for one more year. In that stillness there was the low shriek, the roar of phantoms, like banshees, like dybbuks screaming overhead just above red tiled rooftops, wave after wave of fighter planes that peel off just above the kibbutz, shattering hope for the reprieve just after one o'clock, some heading north to the Golan, others rolling to their right over on their sides down to Sinai, down to the Sea that Moses crossed that once swallowed up Egyptians and would run red again, this time with the blood of Jews, Jews I knew, Jews I loved, comrades in arms, asshole buddies, high school pals, chums, mates, homies, brothers and fathers, husbands of friends, brothers of friends, lovers of friends, friends of friends, and family of family, blown to bits and all of it before it was supposed to be. Somebody broke the deal.

Somebody broke the promise, the terms of the agreement that said there would be Yom Kippur, a day for atonement, a day when you could act before the bullet that would strike you down or the bomb that would rip your flesh, burning phosphorous white and yellow and red, dropping off your bones screaming, whistling like the devil's own ram's horn, *that* was the deal! We had a time-out here! We had a King's X here! Our foot was still on the base! That was the deal between us and God, that fate wouldn't be sealed till the shofar sounded. Not the F9 Phantoms that shrieked overhead, not the thousand-pound frog rockets that came flying down upon us later, again and again, not the constant roar of a thousand cannons streaming down the Golan to the shores of Galilee. It was supposed to be the shofar, a long blast, Takiyah Gedola, one long mighty triumphant hopeful blast that said it's over. But there was no shofar's blast.

Just the planes and then the beep, beep, beep, beep of the radio and the announcer's voice that said, "This is the voice of Israel from Jerusalem," and you knew that it was judgment. When God takes you out of the synagogue on Yom Kippur he doesn't do it so you can come back again. You heard that sentence time and again from widows' lips, through widows' tears, through sobs and beatings of breasts, rending of cloth, breaking of hearts and dreams and hopes and most of all, the promise that there would be a day for atonement, and somebody broke the deal. The question is, was it man or God? Which brings me back to Detective Chan and her notion of when the rich Haole lady's fate was sealed.

If you recall, she said it was the minute the future husband and murderer laid eyes on her. My guess is, it was before that. At least it was for Nora. Remember I said it started with the woman? Well, her name was Nora and like I said when we started this thing, if you feel the need to pinpoint the exact moment when things took an irrevocable turn down the road to somebody being killed, it was long before Nora ever laid eyes on the boy toy who would ace me out for the job of murdering her husband. The moment when all their fates were sealed was long before she ever saw the boy, or me for that matter. Rather, it was when Nora McKinney felt the itch . . . and decided to scratch.

Thirty-seven or thirty-eight is a perfect age for a woman. There's danger there, the body's still firm where it ought to be and soft where it has to be, there is no more pretense at innocence, which where sex is concerned is a highly overrated commodity anyway. The rose is no longer a dewy bud holding tight to its promise, rather it is in full long-petalled sweet high-test perfumed blood-red and glorious bloom. Blood red did I say? And wine red and sweet ripe flesh red, so red you can feel it soft beneath your fingers, on your lips and on your tongue. And the danger you well may ask? What is that? It's there, mon vieux, for the sniffing. Take a whiff beneath the perfume: a hint too sweet perhaps, past seductive and not quite pungent. That smell: loamlike, primeval, like the jungle floor of a rain forest that speaks not to Judeo-Christian anything, a pagan smell that mixes new life and decay, the birth of hope and death of illusion, the same egg that could have hatched a fluffy chick that now has turned to rot, the slightly sulphurous smell of Pele, Dante, Haleakala, and hell, the past-ripe fig split open, left drying in the sun, the hairy pit of life that's begun to smell unclean, this woman at the height of her own beauty, at the peak of her own powers, feeling full tilt all the obsessive driving passion of her own appetites unleashed, unbound as Janis Joplin hair blowing back on a windy mountain, that woman, so full of life, can smell in the air around her, her own impending, ever so slowly slight . . . decay. The wrinkle here, the sag there, the gray hair, the dimpled thigh, the breast that's not so perky, the nipple once pink, now brown . . . *The liver spot!*

Worse for a beautiful woman, don't you know. Worse by far for a woman used to eyes following, tongues hanging out, woodies stiffening under Levis or Armanis, so much worse for one who would have traded as Nora surely did for what, two decades, on her beauty. No. Longer than that. Do the math yourself. She's what . . . thirty-seven, thirty-eight? How long has she been beautiful? Beautiful and sexy since she was sixteen? Fifteen?

I can see her at fifteen . . . have mercy. Take that beauty and let it learn men's secret sighs, their numb-nutted droolings, their oh-baby-yeahs and you-bitch-do-this . . . and that . . . and that . . . take that beauty and give her twenty years to thrill to it, be embittered by it, be bored with it, learn to trade upon it, trade up on it, from backseat to beach shack, from beach shack to condo, condo to penthouse to ocean-front real estate in paradise, looking pristine, fronting deals if not with the devil then with the devil's friends. Let her learn the price of beauty and raise it, only to see the newer models with dewy flesh and upturned tits strut their stuff like she can't quite do anymore . . . not like before. But what the hey, a striptease is better than naked, right? The experienced tongue that knows just where to lick and how and when, the learned nibble, and hungry eye . . . those things are not chopped liver, n'est-ce pas? Dirty old men may like nubile cheeks in Catholic school checks and white knee socks, but take a boy . . . any boy, young and firm and in his twenties who thinks like all boys do (only with his dick) and turn a woman loose upon him, not a girl who needs her coaxing and coquetting, not a teeny, nor a coed, nor a twenty-something yuppie stuffed with angst and just past acne, but a long-legged, gym-hardened, full-breasted, fire-breathing, by God hot-damned, horny-assed, full-blossomed, no-mo'-bullshit, give-it-to-me-hard-and-bring-your-friends-down-too type woman and well . . . what can I say . . . *putty!* A lox being led by his woody, his stiff resolve soon turned limp only to rise once more beneath the tutor's knowing touch and tickle.

That was the boy. That was Chad, golden-skinned and little golden hairs downy soft; brown-gold skin like juicy turkey straight from the oven, the kind that's wet with juice beneath the knife and on the tongue; the muscled arms; the dark hair turned blond from beach or bottle; the stubble beard and cut pectorals; the dolphin glide along his ribs; the muscled stomach and bulge in his baggies; the surfer knots at kneecaps and graceful man-boy walk, athletic and erotic and innocent and just plain nasty; the lungs too young to give way to nicotine; the muscles taut not from exercise but youth, the physical state of unearned grace of physical perfection—in spite of fast-fried grease palace cuisine, jug wine, warm beer, and Maui hemp. He works as a waiter here or there for a month or six, till he gets fired or quits or just doesn't show up, only to turn up down the street in a new joint just like the first. He worked at Longhis, worked the hotels, the beach boy, cabana boy, pool boy, deckhand on the trimaran, until the girl he was shtupping, the cute-as-a-button, hot-as-a-pistol Mormon girl who looked like pre–Billy Joel Christie Brinkley got him the job at Kimo's.

He worked the tables till he got the job at the bar. *That* was where the action was.

Not for money.

Christ, if this kid wanted money he'd have gone to college and made some by now. No, this hunk of meat is interested in party time. Party time might just last another ten years, maybe even fifteen before he looked like Slade, the forty-year-old with beer gut, sagging pecs, and nicotine skin. But when you're twenty-five and shtupping someone new every night, and surfing someplace new every dawn, diving, drinking, smoking, screwing, plenty good fun partying . . . there is no forty. There will never be a you that's forty, just the party.

And if you need money?

That's why God made tips.

That's why God made dope, so you could sell it to the college kids, the locals and the Haoles. Selling dope on Maui is easy. So is sex. So is finding a party. What else is there?

And when you start to think like that . . . like . . . what else is there? Like . . . hey, bra . . . like what else is there . . . you might just find it.

Some find it and get married. They put a ring on its finger, watch it get fat and sassy, pregnant, and boom, Jack! You got a little dude and a full-time job and bills and shit like that, and some guys stick it out and some guys don't. Some guys like the family, like cookin' in them big pots for all the relatives and friends who come by Pau Hana, when work's over, not much money, but oh honey . . .

And some guys bail and start the party all over again, but this time they are fatter and so are the girls. That's okay, get drunk enough and tell yourself and them you're built for comfort not for speed.

Other guys . . . they go back mainland, back to the world, looking for normal. Not Chad. When he started thinking, or what passed for thinking . . . like what else is there, bra . . . he saw Nora.

She was watching.

She'd been watching for a while, like a pussycat licking its chops.

She wore something white and long that slid down hips and opened with a slit, that went back up and opened wide when she crossed her legs and pulled the slit closed, then looked him in the eye and let it fall again and slide up inside her thigh as she looked him in the eye, let honey-blond hair hang low across one sleepy, heavy lidded eye that held him there, cat's paw–like. It made his scrotum tighten.

What does Mister Suave do? What does the Cary Grant of old Lahaina do after having been flashed by the single most primo hunk of fluff between here and Bangkok? He walks over like Mortimer Snerd and says, "Uh . . . hi."

She leans in toward him. "When I was seventeen I met an Italian with a Ferrari. He raced them for a living. He took me for a drive on some godforsaken twisting road in the Pyrenees. Up until that time I thought the most exciting thing in the world that you could do with a car was race a Ferrari through the Pyrenees with thousand-foot drop-offs an inch or two away. But he told me I was wrong. He told me it was far more exciting to sit in the passenger seat, lean back your head, let the wind blow through it, and surrender to the fact that now your own life and death was completely out of your control and in the hands of another. That's where the real excitement was . . . not in control. The real excitement . . . was surrender."

Chad could not help but gulp and sneak a peek down her dress at the perfect cleavage, the perfect breasts in their silky cocoon that gave like a sigh as she breathed.

"Is that what you did?" he asked. "You surrendered?"

"No," said Nora with just the tiniest hint of a smile on her perfect full fleshed lips that parted seductively when she said, no, as if *no* was the most seductive word in the world. "No," she said, "I went down on him."

Her eyes fastened upon his own, like enemy radar locking on your fiery tail just before the missile flies and tracks you to certain death.

"You see," she said, "I like being in control. You're the one who ought to surrender."

She sucked at her mai tai with those perfect lips and let just a drop of rum run down her finger before she licked it off. "It'll be the ride of your life."

"Now then," she said later, back at his apartment, her fingers expertly slipping loose the buckle on his belt, her lips brushing up against his ear. "Isn't this better than trying to think of something smart to say?"

And later if the boy had perhaps a literary eye, maybe he would have seen the diamond-framed Cartier panther resting on his Formica, and maybe he would have thought how oddly sexy it looked there, gold and diamonds crouching on his thrift-store table by the window, where the lights of Front Street peeked in between his curtains, and somewhere in the distance slack key island reggae died and vanished, mistlike in the night.

Did he ask her name? Did he already know it? Had she let it slip like a silk slip sliding down her torso, or had he been smart and kept his mouth shut? Had he surrendered even then? Had he said to himself, If this is the price, I'll pay it? Had he even made that calculation? Would he have had the strength to even think?

I didn't. I just lay there in the darkness, nostrils filled with the smell of her, the taste of her, the scent of her all over me, thinking . . . I had no idea . . . I had no idea what this could be like. I had no idea this was even possible. This wasn't sex, this was near death, isn't that what they call it . . . a near death experience when your soul gets sucked outside, vacuumed out, whooshing into darkness through the blackened tunnel like a sports car plunging, like a spirit in the darkness into birth and light and floating on the scent of her and her

perfume, newborn puppy weak and laughing like
a loon, howling without a sound as she cups you in
her hand and brings you back to life. If the kid was
smart, he kept his mouth shut. Because what interested her wasn't anything he had to say. If the
kid was like me, he would've surrendered and then
she would have told him of her husband. He was
rich. Filthy rich. Fabulously filthy rich.

"He beats me."

Well no shit, I thought. What else is she going
to tell me after the third time we've made love,
with the fumes of dead bottles of Bacardi creeping
up off the floor? What else is she gonna tell me,
that she's really happily married, the proud mother
of three, that she works at the school hot lunch
program and chairs the PTA? No shit she's married to a guy who beats her and treats her just like
dreck, what else would she be doing here? Or
maybe . . .

"Because you want him to?"

"Fuck you," she says.

"Fuck me," I said, my throat gone hoarse and
dry. "Fuck me," I said. I whispered it. I prayed it.

She would have told Chad of her horrible husband.

"He's almost sixty," she said. "He's a bastard."

Almost sixty, the kid would have thought, Jesus
he's an old bastard. He's like, what . . . twenty,
twenty-two years older than her?

"He degrades me," her voice so soft and far
away. "Humiliates me." Little girl–like, almost for

the first time, frightened. She turns and looks at him and those eyes now, those laser-beam, cobalt panther eyes are bloodshot now and tearing, welling up and over and spilling down her cheek. "Do you mind if I talk?" she says. "Please?"

The kid watches her. She's vulnerable now for the first time and then dry and hard again.

"I have any number of people I can sleep with. I have no one I can talk to."

"Sure," he says, "go ahead."

What's he gonna say, what's he gonna say to every boy's wet dream come to life there beside him, with Lahaina lights playing pink and rosy across her skin.

"He's pimped me."

"What do you mean?"

"What does it sound like I mean?" her voice harsh and sharp as a Sunset whore, then soft again, childlike, wounded, hiding, hiding in the darkness there beside him.

"The first time he drugged me and I woke up in our bed underneath this wheezy old bastard who was drooling on my neck."

"He drugged you and gave you to one of his friends?"

"No, to one of his enemies. He said I was dessert . . . at a business meal."

She's quiet, then on fire, flaming in the darkness as she sucks in on the cigarette that glows there, bounces there in darkness beside him, and sighs out smoke, along with her perfume.

"There were others after that . . . and then there were his toys."

"Why do you stay with him?"

There! Stop the tape right there, the Barry Sheck–like voice inside his head should have screamed out. What's *that*, Mr. Fung, its nasally voice should have shouted. Right there, you putz! You schmuck! The hook is being planted! Don't you see it? Don't you feel it? The minute you say, Why do you stay with him, you've opened the door to why not leave? And why not leave with me. You and me together.

She laughed low and throaty, startling, so out of place here, so raspy in its sound. "For the money," she says, as if he's a slow-witted child, which of course he is. "For the money. Why else would I stay with him? He's a degenerate and he's sixty; he's bound to die."

"Why don't you just divorce him and take half the money?"

"Because I signed a prenup even God couldn't break."

Well thank my lucky stars and garters I'm a Jew. When I hear about deals that God can't break, I know who they're made with.

And maybe she could see it on me, see it in my eyes that I would balk at going up that street, that the journey (if made at all) might not be worth the effort, not with me.

But the boy was something else again. The boy

was as the name implies . . . a boy, thinking with his dick.

She swallowed him whole, haunted his days, not just his nights, turned his tanned skin pale, and left him baying at the moon. She shtupped the living shit out of this kid and the more he had the more he wanted, not wanted . . . needed, needed more than he'd ever needed anything in his life. Needed her like drowning men need air. Well you know what they say about Maui . . . it's an island; a small island at that. And in that sense, it's very much like a kibbutz, where everyone knows what color your underwear is and who is shtupping whom, who's the shtupper and who's the shtuppee . . .

Nora's husband was a wolf-eyed gent who at sixty, still had strength, still had power, still had the scent of murder about him that went with all the island stories of the men he'd killed in other countries in his youth. He had built his house on dead men's money.

He did not get to be sixty by being dense. It was perhaps one of the qualities that made him so oddly attractive to beautiful women. His attentiveness . . . his curiosity. He was a sponge. He would soak you up. He wanted to know all about you. He made you feel as if no person on the face of the earth had ever been as fascinating as you.

And of course he had spies.

And they had cameras.

They brought him pictures, long-lensed, secret prying pictures of their bodies, his wife and the lithe young boy, so powerful-looking where his own flesh had gone to rot, of the look on his wife's face which he had never seen.

He looked at them dispassionately, with an amused expression but certainly not without interest . . . great interest.

Two

Wait a second. What kind of schmuck would look at naked pictures of his wife en flagrante coitus enjoyus with a well-hung cabana boy, dispassionately with an amused expression, albeit with the aforementioned great interest? The great interest part is understandable. Who wouldn't have at least a passing interest in pictures depicting your quarter-century younger wife shtupping the local stud muffin? One could imagine that even the most jaded of personalities would express an interest in that. Great interest would certainly be normal on the part of the husband, any husband. And Jack Wolfe was definitely not just any husband.

Word had it that Wolfe was a German Jew

whose businessman father had fled Berlin in the thirties for the relative safety of Shanghai. There the elder Wolfe opened an import/export business. Wolfey Senior belonged to a small group of European Jews who made their way to China just before Adolf went into the soap business. They were mainly Russian Jews, or Ukrainian Jews who came later, who made the long trip on the railway cars and wound up in that island of opium-induced capitalism sitting on China's coast like a European sphinx in drag, crouching on her haunches where the Yangtze sent clumps of human dung and bloated corpses with its commerce to the sea.

They huddled in the less-than-protective shadow of the European concessions, some living on hocked jewels sewn into coat linings, while others worked for the concessions as accountants, bookkeepers, lawyers, business types. Some were hired to tutor the concessionaires' children in all that Europe had to offer at a time when all Europe really had to offer them was a choice in how to die. They tutored rich Chinese in French and German. One of Europe's greatest impresarios became a maître d', a former professor who specialized in Goethe became his waiter.

People sold art, knowledge, jewels, furs, heirlooms, memories; the precious trinkets that were ghosts of a Europe that was finished with them. They opened businesses. They lived in poverty until they were interned with the other European noncombatants in Japanese detention camps.

When it was over, Wolfe the elder took his wife and son first to Hong Kong, then Saigon. After he died, Wolfe Junior bounced around Southeast Asia until the sixties, when somehow handsome Jack came up with American citizenship papers. There were rumors of drug sales, arms shipments, CIA connections, and murder. Then, fortune in hand, Jack turned up in Lahaina, a real-estate developer with big-time Asian money behind him. He was the middle man who brokered the deals that built the shopping centers and high rises that sprouted like pig bristles where Hawaiian royalty once frolicked. And if anyone tried to kapu Jack Wolfe, word was he kapued them first.

He laundered money for the tongs and the Yakuza, went the stories, the Jewish laundry boy to the Oriental mobs. He had a connoisseur's eye for women and when he came back from Vegas with Nora as his wife, it seemed to make sense to one and all. He was legit now, the story went, or maybe he had never really been bent. Any successful businessman had enemies. People talk stinks bruddah, leave it alone.

Then one night at the bar at Longhis, Nora wore the white slit dress and her golden skin and told me about the Ferrari ride through the Pyrenees, and later, when I wondered who do I have to kill to possess this woman, she made it plain that it was her husband. Truth is, I never liked him. Maybe I could just arrest him. Get him on something. Book 'em Dano, deport him. Paradise is that kind of place. I knew a nice little Japanese gardener, a grandfather type who lived in terror that one day, Haole cops or Feds or soldiers would come and say, "You're the one who got away. You're the Jap from the two-man sub that went aground December 7th, 1941 and declared a separate peace, left your dying shipmate and melted into paradise." He had no papers. He barely spoke English. He trusted no one. He had no idea if he was a traitor or a spy. He lived the life of a cockroach. He vanished in the dark.

So maybe there was something on Jack Wolfe. Maybe something that went back to Saigon or Shanghai. I couldn't ask Joan Chan or anyone else in the department, since I had not altogether ruled out the notion of murdering him myself.

But there was one guy who might be able to give me some answers, and what he didn't know, I knew he could find out.

My Uncle Izzy.

Izzy "Machine Gun" Kahana.

My Uncle Izzy, né Israel, nicknamed Srulik in the old country, was about ninety-five or a hundred. No one knew for sure. He couldn't remember and there was no one left alive to ask. He'd outlived them all. Uncle Izzy came to Canada just before World War I. He was a big kid for his age, could pass for an adult. Now at that time, the

Canadians figured they had all the Jews they needed in the Eastern provinces. But out West was something altogether different. There were few white people out West in Alberta; mainly there were Blackfoot Indians. The Schvartze Fissellach, my uncle Izzy called them. So the government told the immigrants they could have a piece of land or a loan to start a general store if they just agreed to head for the hinterland. Uncle Izzy said he knew nothing about farming, so he took the loan. He opened a general store and extended credit to all the ranchers. Then he foreclosed on them. By 1925, he was one of the biggest cattle ranchers in Western Canada. That's when he got my dad out of an Italian prison into which he'd been put for violation of Italy's immigration laws. My dad was traveling without benefit of papers, trying to get to what was then Palestine, having walked from Russia to Milano, where he was arrested and set to be deported back to the worker's paradise and a death sentence passed in absentia for counterrevolutionary Zionist activities. So Uncle Izzy sent the money to bribe the prison officials, get the forged passport, pay for the steamship tickets, and bring his only brother to Canada.

My dad said, "I don't know how I can ever repay you."

"How *do* you intend to repay me," his brother asked, now that my father had broached the subject.

My dad said he didn't know. He would get a job.

My uncle told him no one would hire him. He spoke no English, only Russian, Yiddish, Hebrew, Aramaic, and Ukrainian. He had no real skills. Who would hire him? My uncle Izzy went on to say that he was used to getting a return on his investments. My father owed him not only the money his brother had so generously advanced but the interest it would have earned in a bank as well.

So my father went to work for his brother as a ranchhand, an indentured servant on his brother's ranch. They never spoke again. Except once. My father caught the woman he was in love with, a French-Canadian woman who worked as a cook on the ranch and who was, like my father, an indentured servant. He caught her shtupping a Polish cattle buyer in the backseat of a Model A.

My father said nothing to the woman. Her name was Mimi, I later found out. My father had hidden away a picture of her which I found after he died. It was inscribed, "For my Mishka. I love you always, Mimi."

Anyway, my father said nothing to her. He just walked up to the big house where his brother with whom he had not spoken in three years lived. There was a poker game going on. Uncle Izzy was a compulsive gambler. He used to play every Thursday night with a Blackfoot Indian chief who had made a fortune in the oil business and a Scots-man named MacDonald and the big ham-fisted Ukrainian who owned the slaughterhouse and smelled always of blood. My dad, who at the time made twenty-seven dollars a month plus room and board, said there was fifty-thousand dollars on the table. One hand, fifty thousand. Well, it was the twenties.

My father told his brother he wanted to talk to him.

"There's a game going on, Mishka," was all Uncle Izzy said to him.

My father told him this wouldn't take long. He wanted the French-Canadian woman, Mimi, off the ranch and sent back to Montreal on the morning train. My father would work off what she owed.

"That's it?" asked Uncle Izzy. "That's what couldn't wait?"

"That's it," my father said.

"She owes two more years on her contract," Izzy told him, never looking up from his cards.

"I'll work them off," my father said. And he did.

"Your father was a schmuck," my Uncle Izzy told me, adding quickly, "I loved him. I loved him more than anyone in my life. But he was an ideal-istic romantic putz. Just like you. Full of nar-ishkeit."

"I need some information, Uncle Izzy," I told him.

"So go call four-one-one. I'm an alter yid. El viejo gringo judeo who shoots rats from his front porch. What do I know?" Uncle Izzy knew plenty.

He'd gone broke after the stock market crash. Lost everything except the one little ranch that he'd put in my father's name. There were other things, too. He had gone public with one of his ranches, sold shares and embezzled to cover gambling debts. He got out of Canada one step ahead of the Mounties on a freighter bound for the Orient. In Macao, he'd jumped ship and taken a job as a bodyguard after one sharp-eyed Chinese officer had seen the way he handled himself in a barroom brawl. He became a mercenary in the Kuomintang army. In the thirties, he smuggled arms for Chiang Kai-shek. And planes and parts, bullets and bombs for Claire Channault. He was probably the only Jew in the world who could translate from Mandarin to Blackfoot. He knew Shanghai like the back of his hand. He had a mistress there until the Japanese took the city. She bore him two sons. My two cousins. Two Chinese kids named Kahana. I asked him about Jack Wolfe.

"Why do you want to know?" he asked. He looked me up and down.

"It has to do with a woman," I said.

"What a putz," he said. "Just like your father."

Jack Wolfe's father, Uncle Izzy said, had been the owner of a cabaret in the Fatherland when he saw the writing on the wall that said "Juden" in sulphur yellow letters, so he left with his wife and mistress and sought refuge in Shanghai where he had ties to the Kuomintang through the local mob known as the Green Gang, and one Green gangster in particular by the name of Big Eared Tu. "Big Eared Tu," my Uncle Izzy said, "was one kenna-hora Chinaman."

Big Eared Tu offered Wolfey Pere a little concession of his own: to become the purveyor of the most beautiful European women in Shanghai to the Chinese gangsters, since it was well known that the wealthy Westerners preferred Asian girls. Well, the grass is always greener, right? Payment was not in money, since no one with any sense placed any faith in any country's monetary system, not with a war on, not with armies deciding what was paper and what was worth killing for. No, payment would be in a more stable currency: opium. Opium, Wolfey Pere knew well, could be sold anywhere, even back in dear old Deutschland, and more important, Wolfey Senior knew that opium was something else . . . it was the future. War was a temporary thing. Narcotics were forever. They represented the only thing victor and vanquished had in common.

The desire to anesthetize oneself, to blot out what horrors you had done to others, what horrors they had done to you.

The future lay in annihilating the mind, wiping out memories, eliminating the past and making the present numb enough to bear for the guiltiest murderer or for the most guiltless survivor.

"Everybody's got something that keeps them up at night," my uncle Izzy said. "Everybody has their own little packelach of ghosts and dirty laundry." No matter which side your karmic bread was buttered on, opiates were both the teaspoon of medicine *and* the sugar that made it all go down just fine.

Think how little Wolfey had been raised listening to his father wheel and deal, hustle and pimp.

"Tu, my friend," Papa Wolfe would have said, "you're sitting on one of the most valuable commodities in the world but you're selling it to Chinamen . . ."

And to the women? "What can it hurt? Who's ever going to know? These are Chinamen. Who talks to them? And they're refined cultured people . . . where will you get money like this? Think of your children. It's noble what you're doing. You're a saint and an angel . . . and you get to indulge in secret pleasures, a belle du jour, the White Goddess worshipped by heathens and they know things, these Chinamen, secrets of the flesh, and who will ever know? I'm not saying make a habit. Once . . . that's all . . . for your children, and no one will ever know."

"Then he took their pictures," my uncle Izzy said. "There was a crawl space in the ceiling of the room he used. He sent his kid up there with a Leica, nice camera. The kid would take the pictures. This one you're asking me about now? Wolfe Junior? He would take the pictures. Then his father had them, the women. He owned them after that. Only one or two ever committed suicide."

And the others? Well he had the opium didn't he? He had the sugar to make the medicine go down.

"Perpetua mobile," Uncle Izzy said savoring the Latin sounds. "The women get the drugs and the drugs get the money and the money gets the power and the women."

"This guy was a Jew?"

"Half Jew, half German. Worst of both. He was one of those people you see who had fallen, and he couldn't live with the idea that there was anyone who wouldn't have fallen just as he had, couldn't live with the idea that there could be a person who couldn't be corrupted as he had been. And so he had to corrupt any piece of purity he saw, any piece of goodness, because if there was someone who could live through what he had lived through and not be corrupted, what was his excuse, huh? So maybe you could say he corrupted people out of self-defense, so everyone would be as rotten as him and then he could say, Well, I'm no worse, you're no better. Why put on airs? Wallow in it. We're all hazers. But that's not true. It's a lie the devil tells. Anyway, it came back to bite him in tuchusarein."

"How so?"

"Wolfey Junior killed him. Killed the old man, took over the business, went to Hong Kong and then to Vietnam after the French were kicked out, and smuggled drugs with Tony Marcellus out of Laos and Thailand. That's how he got his citizenship papers. That's who your Jack Wolfe is. This isn't some Polish cattle buyer in the back of a Model A. This is a devil and the son of a devil."

"Hello, Lovey," said Jack Wolfe. "You look positively flushed. Have an exciting day?"

He was wearing what Nora called his Nazi-in-the-tropics suit. White linen pants and a silk shirt unbuttoned down to his gut, which protruded from his frame like a woman six months pregnant or a tumor. His hair was greasy grey, thinning, pulled back into a ponytail that Gustie, his pet Chihuahua liked to nip at. Who in his right mind would keep a senile Chihuahua, who looked like a bug-eyed rodent and smelled like death now that he was incontinent, and call the thing Gustav, or Gustie, much less put him on the table and let him eat from the same plate?

"Come here, Gustie," Jack would say through teeth that clenched a dog biscuit.

He'd lean forward and let the rat dog nibble the yummy from his own lips.

"Yah, Gustie," he would say. "Now piss off."

"That dog is disgusting," Nora said, trying to get through the room as quickly as possible.

It was a beautiful room, all white with shutters that collapsed plantation style one into the other and opened up on a view of Wailea Point with the lights of Lahaina far off, twinkling down the coast like cheap jewelry on velvet.

"Sit down, Lovey," Jack said, and the rat dog shivered at the tone both he and Nora knew too well. "Not you, Gustie. I meant Mommy."

Nora stopped as if yanked back by a leash.

"What?" she said.

"Don't look at me with big eyes frightened like that," he said in Nazi baby-talk. "I won't bite, will I Gustie?"

"Talk to me or the dog. Make up your mind."

Jack turned to Gustav. "Ooh," he said. "It's Mommy's time of month."

He got up and crossed towards her, dropping the dog, who yelped slightly at the fall.

"Is it your time of month, Lovey?" He looked her up and down. "No, I don't think so . . . you have a certain glow. Flushed? Didn't I say so?"

Nora avoided his look and slid the silver slave bracelet farther up her arm. "I was working out," she said.

Jack ran his index finger down her neck and onto her breast like a naughty boy scooping chocolate off a cake. Then he licked his finger. "Dewy . . . positively dewy." He touched her shoulder with the point of his finger, firmly turning her around like a nun pointing you into a corner. He appraised her like livestock.

"The workout does you good, Lovey. Your buttocks are firm. Nice for a woman your age. Nice and juicy, like a roast." He smacked his lips. "A rump roast."

"Are you through?" Nora said, no longer bothering to hide the revulsion at his touch.

"Yah, well . . . thhhat's the problem, isn't it?" he said, with his fat "th" sound, tongue protruding well past his front teeth every time he said thhhat.

"Thhhat's exactly the problem," he said, pushing her back into the room with one bony finger against her shoulder blade. "I may in fact be thhhrough . . . which of course would mean your future might just be a little droopy too, eh? Shall I make you a drink?"

He crossed over to the white-on-white enamel bar set off in a corner beneath an oh so slowly turning rattan ceiling fan . . . a keepsake from his father's brothel. The rat dog trotted along beside him.

"Vodka?" he asked, almost cheerily. "No, bad news calls for whiskey. Here . . . I give you Bushmill's. Just the way you like it, eh, Lovey?"

He pushed the drink towards her, a stiff shot of Irish whiskey straight up in a short glass. Then he bent like a vulture and scooped the rat dog up onto the bar top.

"He likes the macadamia nuts. Don't you, Gustie?" he said, and took a handful of nuts from the black lacquer bowl. "But he doesn't have the teeth for them anymore."

With that, Jack took one of the nuts, put it between his teeth, chomped it neatly into bits, spit them in his palm like a mother bird regurgitating dinner and held it out to the toothless Chihuahua.

Nora took a long slow sip of the Irish whiskey. "What exactly do you mean, you're through?"

"The money, you know? Kaput. And that's the least of it." He put another nut between his teeth, chewed it into a kind of macadamia mash and spit into his palm, as Gustie licked his chops and wagged his stub.

"I know it may shock you, Lovey, and I Pray to almighty God it doesn't change your opinion of me, but I'm afraid my accounting practices have been less than legal. A finagle here, a finagle there . . . the last two shopping centers . . . belly up. And of course, the fact that we're publicly traded now means the SEC and the rest of their jack-booted thug accountant types will be breathing down our necks . . . awful really."

Nora had not taken her eyes off him, watching like a mongoose watches a snake. "How awful?"

"Ah, mein kleine frau, always so concerned about your hubby's welfare. Touching really. That's why, you know, as long as I have you and Gustie by my side . . ."

"How awful, Jack?" Nora said, leaning forward now, the fear just there behind her eyes, on the sharp edge of her voice.

Jack took it in at a glance and had he been

blind, he would have known it. He could smell it on her. Jack could smell fear on women more easily than perfume. And for him of course, it was a far more seductive scent.

"Well I wanted to spare you of course," he said, "but since you insist." He pulled a gold cigarette case from his pocket, pulled a Gauloises cigarette from its place in line with all the other cigarettes standing at attention like a firing squad. He tamped the tobacco down against the cigarette case, put the cigarette between his lips, and then softly spit a fleck of tobacco at the dog.

"Do you have a light, Lovey?"

Nora fished into her purse, which she had tossed on the bar the night before. She pulled out a book of matches and slid them across to Jack, who took in the printing on the side as he lit his vile-smelling French tobacco.

"Kimo's," he said, reading the name on the matches. "Such a charming place. So many young people."

"How awful?" Nora said again, mentally kicking herself about the matches.

"Within six months at the most, I should think, we'll have lost everything and I'll be in jail," he said, taking a long, luxurious drag on the cigarette.

For the tiniest moment, there was a glimmer of something in Nora's eyes. Whether it was joy or revenge or hope or what amounts of each was impossible to say.

"You too of course, I'm afraid," he said, and

pulled at a fleck of tobacco stuck to his tongue with his thumb and index finger.

"Me too what?" said Nora. "What are you talking about?"

"Can I freshen your drink?"

"Cut the shit, Jack, and tell me what's going on. What do you mean, me too?"

Jack reached over and poured more Bushmills into Nora's glass. "Just say when, Lovey. Probably a stiff one, eh? I know you like them stiff."

He poured the glass up to the top till the whiskey sloshed over the rim. "You're a corporate officer, you know; it's the age of liberation. Wives don't just bake cookies. So certain things were done in both our names, you know? Whither thou goest, I shall go? And whither *I* goest . . . I'm afraid you goest, too. Can you imagine what a field day those dykes will have with you? God, I'd give anything for pictures." He sighed.

Nora threw the drink in his face. He wiped it off his cheek and licked his fingers. "That's a waste of good whiskey."

"You son-of-a-bitch bastard," she said. "You son of a bitch."

"Come, come," said Jack. "You never even knew my mother. Anyway, you wanted to know what the problem was, that's it. But there's a way out, Nora."

Her eyes flicked towards him in spite of herself, looking for help, for the promised lifeline. For the only hand up out of the quicksand into which he had just pushed her. It was the fulcrum of their relationship—push-pull, torture-scream, the anticipation punctuated by pain.

"You didn't think Daddy was going to leave you in the shit all alone, did you baby?" he said, touching her cheek. "Did you, Lovey?"

"God," she said, "How I hate you."

"I know," Jack whispered. "It's one of your most endearing qualities." He took another drag off the cigarette. "I think you should murder me."

He let that lie there in the air between them.

"I think, Lovey, you should find a boy." He crossed in closer towards her so she could feel his breathing on her neck. "Some tan, muscular empty-headed boy who thinks only with his dick." He ran his hands down against her bare arms.

"You should take him to bed. You're really an exciting piece of ass, you know? A real animal. That's what you should be with him. Get a boy you can destroy. Get him to fall in love with you. This should be nothing for you . . . not with your wonderful buttocks and your beautiful legs. And then you should convince him to help you murder me. I'll even show you how to do it. I'm insured for fifteen million dollars. You tell the boy that when the husband is dead, you the grieving widow will get the fifteen million and live happily ever after with your young Lothario. You like my plan so far?"

"So far," she said drily.

"You see, Lovey, here in Hawaii, it's the most

marvelous thing, but you don't really need a corpse in order to declare someone dead. Sometimes . . . all you need is a murderer." He kissed the nape of her neck and bit softly into her flesh. He was a vampire. He sucked the life out of people. He lived on death.

"So you see, you plot the murder and together we frame the boy. He is caught . . . didn't you know a policeman once? The Jew . . . yes, that's wonderful. You could cry on the shoulder of the Jew. The boy is caught, he's tried, he's found guilty. And the minute he is, the insurance company pays you the money."

Nora watched him as he came around from behind her, swaying like a cobra. "What's in it for you?" she asked evenly.

"A new start and half the money, Lovey. We're fifty-fifty partners," he said.

"If you're dead," she said, and he could almost feel her savor the words, "why should I give you half the money? What would you do if I kept it all, sue me?"

"No," said Jack. He pulled a tape recorder up from behind the bar. She could see the little wheels spinning behind the plastic window. "I simply give the tape of this conversation to the authorities. You won't betray me. Because if, God forbid, I should actually turn up dead, should anything prevent me from notifying a certain friend of mine, someone you don't know, someone you never even

knew existed, someone whom I can trust implicitly, should I not be able to notify that friend that
all is well with me, then that trusted friend will
take this tape to the authorities and you, my darling Lovey, will fry. One other thing. When this is
over, you'll be free of me."

He poured a short whiskey for himself and
lifted the glass till their eyes met above it. "To a little murder then?" he said.

"To a little murder," Nora replied.

She would have rolled that one around in her
mind a time or two. She would have looked at it
from every side, sniffed around its edges, probed
here and there, looking for the trap. Because there
had to be one. On the other hand, what did Jack
have to gain by trapping her? She was already
trapped, bound and branded. She was cattle and
he could do with her as he pleased. They both
knew it. His little rat dog had more freedom. There
was nothing she did that he did not allow and she
knew that, too.

But she had to be certain. Was the trap set just
for Chad, or her too? What if there was more than
one tape recording? But then, she thought, in
order to destroy her, he would have to destroy his
own chances of getting the money. He couldn't ex-
pose her without exposing himself and since she,
Nora, was the sole beneficiary on the policy, how
could he collect if she was in prison? This was vin-
tage Jack. Pure Jack. One hundred percent grain
alcohol, unadulterated, sadistic Jack. Make her be-

tray her lover and save Jack's ass and get him seven and a half million dollars in the bargain, while he watched . . . while he pulled the strings . . . while he took the pictures.

"What's Jack Wolfe got on his wife?" I asked Joan Chan once I had come to terms with the fact that I would not murder Nora's husband for her and so would lose her.

"What do you care?" Joan asked with a bemused expression of her own.

"I was thinking about killing her husband for her," I said as offhandedly as I could. But trying to be inscrutable with Joan Chan was a waste of time.

"What a pits," she said.

"I think that's putz."

Joan shrugged her brown-skinned hula dancer shoulders. "Pits, putz," she said. "What makes you think I know anything about Nora Wolfe?"

On the face of it, that was probably a pretty good question. But then on the face of it, anything to do with police work in Maui could be questionable. Maui County P.D.'s detective bureau looked more like a Holiday Inn than a squad room. For that matter, "plainclothes" in Maui took on a whole new meaning. Here the quickest way *not* to blend in was jacket and tie. The well-dressed detective in Maui wore shorts or Dockers and a luau shirt, and looked more like the bellmen at the

Royal Hawaiian than anything else. But then like I said, even though Joan Chan looked like a hula dancer, she made Serpico look like a wuss.

"I don't know," I said. "A high-profile guy like Wolfe rumored to be fronting for the tongs and the Yakuza? My guess is there's not a lot about him and anything connected to him you don't know."

Joan scooted back in the chair and then I realized this had nothing to do with cops and everything to do with women. She wore a look that said she loved how stupid white guys were.

"You really love her for her mind, right?" she asked, smiling, leaning forward just enough so I could smell the scent of gardenia on her.

"Right."

"Right," she said. "God, are you easy. I thought Jews were supposed to be smart."

"You ever hear of Delilah?" I asked, "The hairstylist who gave Samson a new 'do?"

"Gotcha," said Joan Chan. "She was a hooker."

"Delilah?" I asked.

"Nora Wolfe," Joan said, tossing a paper clip at my head.

"I'm shocked," I said and tried not to think about that one too long, tried to sound too cool for words, like tell me something I *don't* know.

"Fairly high class, if that makes you feel any better," said Joan. "Couple thousand a night. Top of the line Vegas high-roller whore."

She watched me closely, looking for any reaction to her words. You could see she was enjoying this, enjoying how easy guys like me were. She looked like nothing so much as pictures of Yoko watching John. Men were dicks.

"Anyway," she said, "the story I heard from a Vegas cop was that our friend handsome Jack was in town entertaining a couple Japanese investors—"

"Yakuza?" I asked.

"No," she said, "Japanese investors. You know, pocket calculators and Pentaxes? It was when Jack was selling home sites with golf memberships. He'd have four or five guys a month coming over. Then he'd usually take 'em to Vegas to close the deal. Nora was the closer."

"And . . . ?"

"And some guy freaked on her I guess. Started to smack her around. Anyway, the guy's body was found three days later out in the desert with a couple of bullets in his chest. Right after that, a little money got spread around, no charges were filed and Nora became Mrs. Jack Wolfe."

That's when I remembered Uncle Izzy and the Leica and the crawl space. "He probably has it on tape," I said. "The whole thing."

"What makes you think so?" Joan asked, and maybe somewhere there was just the tiniest hint of surprise in her expression.

"Genetics," I said.

Joan was watching me as closely and as carefully as anyone had ever examined me in my life. It was more than a cop's look.

"Denil," she said, "stay out of this."

"Out of what?"

"Someone *will* be dumb enough to try and kill him for her," said Detective Chan. "If Jack Wolfe ever turns up dead, every cop I know on this island is gonna be going after Nora Wolfe and whoever she's shtipping, faster than Fuhrman went over the gate at OJ's. And trust me, on this island no one's gonna cry racism."

"I think you mean shtupping."

"Shtipping, shtupping," said Joan Chan. "Just feel lucky it's not you."

"You'd arrest me, huh?" I asked smiling weakly, trying to change the subject.

"If I didn't shoot you first," she said. "Just to put you out of your misery."

That night I went home and got drunker than I'd been in a long time and thought about my father and thought about what it was that made immigrants so much smarter than native born. He'd not only been smart enough not to marry Mimi, but he had been smart enough to see through my mother and marry her anyway. He was forty when he left the ranch just before World War II began. His brother had long since flown the coop and he had worked for himself all through the Depression and managed to save up three thousand dollars.

And now with middle age upon him, he decided it was time to find a wife.

He asked a friend of his where the best-looking women in North America were and the guy told him, no doubt about it . . . Southern California. So Mishka Kahana, short, bald, and barrel-chested, with calloused hands and rope-burned palms, headed south with his life savings, a wad of three thousand dollars tucked into his pocket. He was not afraid of being robbed. He was the toughest man I ever knew.

He met my mother in a bar in Long Beach. There was a party going on, some kind of Jewish singles mixer and my father saw her across your basic crowded room. She was twenty-five, dark-haired, and gorgeous. Unlike my dad, who came from twelve generations of impoverished rabbis, my mom came from money. Her grandfather was a baron, one of the only Russian Jewish nobility around.

The family left when they became enemies of the people and my mother grew up with tales of former riches ringing in her ears.

All her sisters, she would say later, had married for love and wound up poor as church mice. She would not make the same mistake. She was marrying for money. What she was looking for, and she made no bones about it, was a rich old man. The richer and older the better, preferably in ill health if she could find one, in which case she would help him die happy. She was not only the best-looking woman in the bar, she was the best-looking woman my father had ever seen, had ever heard of, had ever imagined.

"Chello," he said, with his thick Russian accent. "I can buy you maybe a drink?"

My mother looked him over . . . the barrel chest, the calloused hands . . . the weathered face. This was no Wall Street tan. This was, God forbid, a working man. A wage earner. My mother wasn't interested.

"No," she said. "Thanks but no thanks."

"Sure," said my father, smiling his big, open ranch-hand smile. "Sure, I buy you a drink."

My mother realized he was going to be persistent, so she decided to cut to the chase.

"All right," she said. "You can buy me a drink, if you buy my friends a drink, too, because I don't want you to get the wrong idea about us."

"And what idea would that be?"

"That there *is* an us, because there isn't. And there won't be."

"Okay," said my dad. "I buy the friends a drink, too. Who are the friends?" he said, looking around the room, which held about a hundred people.

"Honey," said my mother with that sly smile and the arrogance arched in her eyebrow, "everybody here is my friend."

"Okay," said Pop. "Drinks are on me."

Whereupon he reached into his pocket and pulled out . . . the wad. Three thousand dollars folding money at the height of the Depression. It looked for all the world to be his pocket change. Immediately my mother's demeanor changed. She went from Jane Eyre to Scarlett O'Hara in a heartbeat.

"What did you say your name was, honey?" she asked, linking her arm through his.

"Mishka," said my father.

"Mishka," said my mother, thinking to herself that it started with the same letter as money. "What a perfectly beautiful name."

They danced, he got drunk, and that night he proposed. In the next six days he blew three thousand dollars on her, and every one of her girlfriends said, "Sweetie, Americans spend when they don't have it, but Europeans? Nev-ver! If that's what he's got in his pocket, he's loaded, sister."

My dad told her he had to go back to Canada to attend to business, which of course was true. He was unemployed, broke, and needed to find a job.

Over the next month they corresponded and my mother gave away everything she owned to her nieces. "Your rich, old maid aunt is going to glory," she told them.

She took the train to Calgary and my father met her at the station. They took a taxi to his home, which was a rented room in a beautiful old Victorian mansion that belonged to a family that had fallen on hard times in the Depression and made ends meet by taking in boarders.

"Well," said my father as the taxi pulled up in

front of the mansion, "it's not much, but this is where I live."

My mother looked at the gables and the leaded glass, the brass fixtures and the windows which promised the fifteen rooms the mansion held inside and said, "It'll do."

He walked her up the steps and opened the door, and there was the rabbi and the wedding canopy and the wedding party, all waiting. My dad was taking no chances. My mother put her suitcase down and got married. They partied and all the boarders drank a toast to the young couple.

Finally my father said, "Well, let's go up to our room."

My mother thought that was an odd way to put it, "our room." And then there was the matter of the guests. They weren't leaving.

"Why should they leave?" my father asked as if butter wouldn't melt in his mouth. "They live here."

Then he closed the door to their room behind him. My mother looked at him and it began to dawn on her.

"What do you mean, they live here?" she asked, hoping he would answer something that would prove he was not only rich but generous. Generosity was a habit she could break him of after all. Poverty was not.

"They rent rooms here," my father said, "just like me."

My mother later said that her plan was simply

to kick him out, spend the night, and get a job the next day. She would stay in Canada for a few months, save the money, and then tell her family that her husband had died and left her penniless. It was one thing to be conned by a corpse, quite another to admit you'd been taken by a ranch hand.

The problem came when she told my father to get out of his own room. My father's logic was simple. "I pay the rent on this room."

My mother's response was equally simple. She slammed the door in his face and locked it.

As I recall from growing up, slamming doors in my father's face was never a good idea. He kicked it open. Neither of them ever said what happened after that, but whatever it was must have worked. They were married for thirty-five years before my father died. Somewhere after that first night, my mother said she grew up and realized what a good man she was already married to.

Looking back on it, my life would probably have been an awful lot simpler if I had never heard that story.

"He wants us to kill him," Nora Wolfe told Chad that night in bed, her naked body glistening in the pink glow of neon that bled in through the window from Front Street down below. She smiled, she giggled like a schoolgirl, like someone in love. "He wants us to kill him. Can you believe that?"

Three

"He knows about us!" Chad yelped, like a puppy who's been stepped on as he sat bolt upright in bed, and truth be known, "sitting" was the only thing bolt upright about him at this point. Everything else that wasn't shriveled from exhaustion was diminished now by abject terror.

"Whoa, shit!" he said as he stumbled out of bed and crossed to the window to lower the blinds, imagining camera lenses, infrared night vision devices, and the crosshairs of a sniper's rifle held by a jealous husband tracing his every move. "Shit, you know?"

He fumbled with the blinds, yanked on the cord, and they came down halfway on one side and not at all on the other.

"Chad," Nora said, in her driest of tones.

"I mean are you sure? He's got like a gun and shit, right? I mean he's some kinda hood or . . . he's like, connected to bad guys, isn't he?"

"Chad, sit," Nora said with a snap to her voice.

Chad was standing by the window, naked, looking down on Front Street at revelers who partied nightly, spilling out of bars, stumbling down past T-shirt shops and gallerys full of posters that said whales were the ones who were in trouble, as they sloshed their Silver Bullets and chugged their Coors and Buds.

One of them who was known to one and all as Dogger looked up and saw the naked Chad.

"Whoa, dude," Dogger exclaimed. "You're naked."

Others looked up to see that indeed he was.

"Whoa," came the incoherent mumble. "Chad's doin' the nasty."

And Chad? Chad couldn't help but look down onto the street full of well-wishers, fans in fact, and smile.

They had cheered once, well not *them*, not specifically them, not the drunks in the street who saw him limp and naked and cheered his exploits, made him their five-second hero before the walking party stumbled down the street and to the shore.

It was other drunks and other times and he was hot, as hot as any kid could be with fingers they said must've been lined with Velcro, so firmly

did he catch the long ball thrown in closing seconds in front of fifty-thousand screaming fans who
hushed and held their breaths and prayed to all
the Gods of Football that he would or would not
catch it. And he could remember it still, exactly
the way it was if not in truth then in his mind. The
sudden hush, the gasp of breath fifty-thousand
strong, the pounding cleats, him and the rubber-
legged black kid straining for position, straining
for the ball, leaning out and forward like race-
horses for the finish, leaving earth, flying up and
over hands outstretched, seeing it there, turning,
spinning before him, and slowing it down with his
mind till he could read the letters.

And it seemed for all the world that he had all
day, could have gone for a snack, could have left
the field and got to his car, gone to a drive-thru, ordered a Big Mac, and still been able to catch the
ball that touched first the tips of fingers and then
rolled down towards him as he squeezed it like a
berry, like a juicy-goosy berry ripe for plucking.
They came down together, his body and the ball
and the black kid there beside him and from the
corner of his eye he saw the ref's hands go upright
and someone punched the mute on the remote
and the sound came up full blast from fifty-
thousand hoarse-voiced lovers.

They were his worshippers and he was
their god.

They were his lovers and he their beloved.

The whole world was him and Mommy and

Daddy and Mommy and Daddy loved him and only him, always him and him alone for all the neat tricks he could do with a ball.

The best that life would ever hold for him if he lived to be a hundred, if he lived a hundred years more, was three seconds on a Saturday afternoon in his twentieth year when he caught a ball. The whole world loved him.

After his knee blew out, the whole world couldn't give a shit.

Those were the other three seconds, when he went up for the pass, got hit on his right, came down on his left leg, and heard the snap like a rifle crack, could swear that he heard it echo throughout the stadium, then saw the blinding light before he felt the pain and then the pain, and then his foot that seemed to be lying there on the ground next to his head. That's odd, he thought, why is my foot next to my head when it ought to be down with my other foot? And then the answer came to him. It's because your knee is destroyed and your foot's just doing whatever the fuck it feels like because it doesn't have a knee to keep it in line anymore.

Chad was one of those people who never learned to speak because speech was never expected of him. He was beautiful to look at, fair of face and clear of eye with the body of an Adonis and skin girls thought was made for licking. Words had never been required. If anything, they broke the illusion.

The thing about being a jock—so I have heard from jocks who told me—was simply this. They get a lot of pussy. It's pretty much the only subject of discussion. First the game. Then the pussy. Some of the brighter ones talk about contracts, but after they get them and the money that comes pouring through the clauses marked Ancillary Merchandising and Endorsements, the conversation turns to pussy. That's why Chad came to Maui. They could take the game away but with a body like his, with the blond curled forelock that hung down into his eyes, they couldn't touch the pussy.

There was still plenty of that. And there were, like now, the occasional cheers of adoration for the former jock who caught the ball that made them gasp on New Year's Day and now stood naked at his window in Lahaina.

"Chad, sit," Nora said.

He sat.

"He's not jealous," she said, trying to break through the film that had glazed across his eyes.

"He's not?"

"Not in any way you could imagine. If anything, he'd probably want to watch."

"Shit," said Chad. Chad was almost Oriental when it came to language. Tone and inflection counted for much more than vocabulary.

"He wants us to kill him."

And Nora told him of the plan, of the fifteen million in insurance, of the fact that in Hawaii you didn't necessarily need a corpse . . . a murderer would do. And for her too, it had come full circle, as she watched the dull and beautiful boy who sat there naked on the bed beside her like the other one, not the first by any means, for that had been reserved for family, but the one she thought about in her adolescent heart of hearts, her rock and roll lexicon of Romeos to her already jaded Juliet, was her tight-jeaned Mick Jagger clone, her very own way out. His name had been Rick.

His jeans were tight, his hair long and greasy black. He had the soul of a poet and the look of Hell's own Angel, she told herself. He was the leader of the pack in a girl-group doo-wop wet dream. He was a junkie.

She was fifteen and a runaway. He was twenty and a musician. He jammed the blues guitar slung low, humping with his hips on the chord change, bending the mike down to him the way she wanted to be bent down to him, neck veins bulging, eyes flashing, singing in that whole room just to her, as if she were the only one there, the only one there for him.

The problem was he was strung out.

He was way strung out. And when the band moved on it moved on without him. His dad was hassling him, get a job, get a job. He had to get out of the house, away from the hassle but he had no money.

And so one time she spoke up, spoke up to Rick's father, to the man she called Mr. Gennaro and said, all fifteen-year-old sweetness and purity,

"Mr. Gennaro, your son's a really beautiful human being with a really beautiful soul. If you wouldn't, you know, trample on it, it would just blossom. I know it would. And you know, he got that soul from you and your wife and from God, it's such a precious thing. You know?"

And he did! He got it. He said maybe the solution would be to fix up the garage into an apartment and Rick could live there. That would give him freedom and yet he wouldn't have to pay any rent. And so they did.

They fixed up the garage, put plasterboard on the walls tacked into the support beams. They put carpet down and bought a lamp, put bean bag pillows on the floor and saved up money till they got a waterbed. It was their own world and it was perfect. And he talked about getting a job and getting married, making babies and having their own house. And for awhile, he was clean, had straightened out, was off drugs. Then it started again, worse than before, though where he got the money she had no idea, since all he did was lay there on the water bed staring at the ceiling, stoned now all the time. When she tried to talk to him about it he hit her, hit her hard and then again in the mouth and broke her jaw, so she went crying to his father, to Mr. Gennaro, who stroked her hair and took her to the doctor and said, "There, there . . . there, there."

Her face was swollen and jaw off center. They told her they would have to rebreak it and set it once again, and it was as if right there in the examining room in one second, one moment, one flash of light, she grew up and saw the world and knew it for what it was.

She had run away from rapists into a nest of rapists. She had what they wanted. It was the only thing she had to trade upon . . . her looks. And the very thing that made her vulnerable to men could, if she learned to use it right, give her power over them.

It was all so clear now, why the father had moved the son into the garage, where the son had gotten the money for the drugs, why the father was not upset to have his addict son stretched out stoned on the waterbed. He wanted her too, and with his son stoned, he could have her, and he did.

So she talked him into taking pictures while they had sex and then said, "Mr. Gennaro, you pay for my fucking jaw, you pay for the plastic surgery, or you're going to prison for statutory rape and corrupting the morals of a minor. Your wife will get these pictures, not just the cops, and I'll tack them up on your parish bulletin board where you go for Mass, you hypocritical guinea piece of shit."

She got the new jaw.

She got the new clothes.

She got the fake I.D.

She got a thousand in cash and a one-way ticket to L.A.

And in L.A. she won the most coveted title of

all . . . fresh meat. She was the new girl at Carlos and Charlie's, she was the one they hadn't seen before at Trumps, she was the one in the after-hours backgammon games upstairs who sat by the Israeli hustler and blew on his dice for luck.

Before long, she was up at Hef's.

She was in the Grotto parties with the producers and the quarterbacks and the comics.

They promised her a centerfold but it never worked out.

Instead, she went with Bernie Kornfeld to Zermatt.

She partied with Koo Stark and Randy Andy.

She blew her nose out on cocaine.

She went with rockers to private islands.

She balled Mick.

And then she got raped in Boca by a German industrialist who she wanted to go to bed with anyway. He broke her jaw again. He paid for the surgery. Said it was worth it. Said he'd like to see her some more. That's when she started carrying the thirty-two.

And then one day she was thirty-five.

Not fresh meat.

Just meat.

Then she met Jack. He listened. He soaked her up like a sponge. He reminded her of Bernie. He reminded her of Mr. Gennaro. He reminded her of her father. She was revulsed and attracted. The revulsion was the attraction. He knew it, too. They both did. He was the punishment and the reward. That was the point. That was the pleasure.

He had a business deal, he said. Japanese businessmen. Big money. Big opportunity. They loved American girls. They loved blondes. They loved that blue-eyed Californian Shiksa Goddess look.

"Christ, Lovey," Jack had said, "if they wanted me, *I'd* go down on them to close these deals."

She demurred.

He persisted.

"Lovey, it's Vegas. We can have so much fun. Didn't you say you used to blow on the Israeli guy's dice? It's the same thing except the payoff is so much better than with some cheap Israeli. You'll be my partner, Lovey. You don't know, my whole life I've been waiting for a woman like you who thinks like me and looks like you. Come on, Lovey, I know what you need."

"It's not what I want," she'd said.

"Lovey," Jack said, kissing her toes, "it's like what that limey with the big lips sang about . . . you can't always get what you want. But I know what you need."

What she didn't need was to be slapped around by some little Nipponese shit who wanted to play Rambo. He hit her, she hit him back. Then he jumped into his little karate stance and said in his Japanese rapper accent, "I mess you up, bitch."

So she shot him. Twice. Dead center, body mass, right in the heart.

"Nice shooting, Lovey," Jack said when he came into the room. "So don't be crazy-assed, you know, put down the gun."

She looked at him wildly, ready to take a few more with her, ready to take them all. Gennaro, Bernie, the Japanese, and Jack . . . she had a bullet for each and every one.

"Lovey . . . ?" said Jack, smiling his Wolfey grin. "Lovey, you hungry? Shall I send out for something? We can clean up the mess later. Come on, Lovey, we go for oysters."

They left the dead guy on the floor and went to the Mirage. Jack tried to talk her into seeing Siegfried and Roy.

"I love those two fairies with the tigers," he said. "Come on, Lovey, you've never seen the white tigers? The dead guy is not going anywhere, that's why they call him dead."

At about the time that Siegfried was joyously plunging sabers into an enraptured Roy, strapped down spread eagle in basic studs and wet black leather, Jack got up and said, "Excuse me, Lovey, I've got to go and drain my lizard."

By the time they got back, the dead guy was gone. The carpet was shampooed, the wall was spackled, and there were flowers. Lilies. Someone had a sense of humor.

Nora was amazed . . . impressed . . . grateful and afraid; all the emotions that Jack treasured.

"One phone call does it all, Lovey," he sang. "It

was a dream, Lovey, a bad nasty dream but Daddy's here and you're safe in my arms once again."

Later that night he showed her the tape.

It was as if he had branded her.

She was his to do with as he pleased.

So in a final act of perversion . . . he married her.

Four

"We'll kill him," she said.

Chad sat there looking at her.

"We'll *really* kill him."

"Whoa," Chad said. "Shit."

"He's going to show us how, and believe me, Jack's the smartest man I know. I've known a lot of people in my life. Jack's the smartest. If he says he can put together a way so it will work, he can. Except instead of faking his death and framing you, we'll kill him and piss on his grave."

She squeezed his hand like a schoolgirl excited about the prom.

"Whoa, shit," said Chad.

"Chad," she said. "Please don't say that anymore."

"Nora, listen," he said as he fumbled around for a cigarette. "I don't know if I'm down for this. I mean, I don't even know him. I mean, I don't even know this guy that you want to kill . . . I mean, shit . . . whoa, you know?"

"Chad," Nora said, crossing to him, her hands drifting south, playing down about his navel, pushing him back towards the bed. "I just told you that Jack was going to frame you for murder and he doesn't know you either. He's scum. It's self-defense. We can be free of him."

"Yeah," said Chad, "But I'm free of him now . . ."

"You think so?" Nora said. "He knows we're here. We're here because he wants us to be here. It's as if he's planned this whole scene out and everything we've said. You could leave right now, we could never see each other again, and Jack would make it look like you did it."

Her tongue licked the salt off his neck and ran down his chest until she found him in the dark and then came back up to him.

"If you don't want to, we won't," she said. "Forget it. Forget I even mentioned it. Except it's fifteen million dollars, Chad. Do you know how much money that is?"

"It's a three-year contract," Chad said in awe. "With a signing bonus."

"It'll be like a game," she said, and her hair fell down and brushed against his skin as she whipped it back and forth and he moved his hips in towards her. "We'll just think about it, we'll just plan it, and if the plan is good, we can do it. And if it isn't, we don't have to, right?"

By then, Chad was incapable of human speech. All he could say was "Yeah . . ."

I saw her coming down the stairs that led to his apartment, down onto Front Street, past the bars and T-shirt shops . . . the way she walked, the way she moved in that slit dress, saw him watching her from up above, from the window where he watched her walk down Front Street and she knew it, too. I could see it on her face, the smile that said she knew she held his eyes.

I watched them after that when she came to his place, when the two of them drove to Hana, when they took the room at Kaanapali, and when Jack was on the mainland and he drove the road to her place, not knowing why or what I'd do about it.

Exquisite torture. Sitting in the car and watching. Down the street from his apartment. Sitting, waiting, smoking, hoping to see her, hoping not to see her, reliving touches and tongues, soft, wet, breathless touches, yes just there, like that, silk slip falling smooth, slipping down her skin, and my tongue and her lips, and her mouth and mine. Remembering it. Feeling it, smelling, touching, aching in my mind there in the car that smelled of ashes overflowing and butts in the bottom of half-drunk cups of coffee, until I saw her. Walking down the street. Wading through the stares of tight-skinned, easy-muscled boys of half my age and half her age, who parted, watched her like a goddess, walking through the natives up the temple steps to hump and bump and grind to the greater glory of Ashtarte, to a cult of Venus that left you drooling, unable to touch, unable to look away.

She felt them watching, soaked up their stares through her skin, her flesh made softer with their staring, her breasts swelling, hips swaying with it, muscles dancing in her thighs. The more they watched, the hungrier they drooled and smacked their lips like toothless winos or puppy studs who thought with dicks. She gathered strength from them, walking up the wooden steps like a goddess to her temple.

I watched their shadow dance, and like her I thought of murder. I parked my car down by the road the night he drove up to the estate when Jack was in the air, leaving paradise, flying like a warlock to the mainland.

I crouch-walked in the moonlight.

Quasimodo by the sea. My footsteps sucked the red-brown mud, the spongy primal soil that spoke of blood and semen rituals of incestuous Polynesian royals, of heads split open with stone cudgels, of half-naked warrior queens, slaughtered babies, murdered lovers, of goddesses who lived in fire and demanded blood.

The air was salty, balmy, humid as a shvitz bod,

velvety soft and indigo blue. Air you could feel, air that resisted when you walked and pushed your way through it like a sweaty crowd.

Dogs barked.

Slack key reggae caught a wave and surfed its way up the beach from far away.

Seabirds screamed, and up on the hill I saw their bodies through the shutter slats in slants of light behind them that cut them, sliced them horizontally a thousand times or more, as he kissed her, bent her back and let the silk slide smooth, gliding down her body to the floor.

I watched them through my gun sight.

I slid the action back and let it slam and thrust the bullet, rip it forward through the metal lips of the ten-round clip into the chamber's hole, the hammer cocked, firing pin poised above the contact point, above the little bud that capped the powder, held them in the V notch, let them do their nasty dance atop the front sight, atop the metal stand-up nub and held in my finger squeeze the blinding flash and the explosion, the white hot spinning steel that screwed its way down through the chamber faster than the sound that spelled their deaths could travel. By the time she heard it he'd be dead. By the time she heard the muffled crack his skull would be ripped open and his blood and brains would be exploding on the white pile carpet and her skin.

All that power, all that blood in a finger's squeeze.

I remember in the army I used to play it like a game, sitting behind my scoped sniper's thirty aught six, training the Syrian in my crosshairs, thinking, You could die right now just because I'm in the mood, sweeping with him as he walked until I saw in the scope the Syrian sniper trained on me.

We watched each other in our sights, in the centers of our crosshairs, each one knowing the muzzle flash meant death was speeding at you faster than you could squeeze your finger. Very slowly I took one hand away from the gun and waved. Very slowly he did the same.

There was no hatred. Just death grins.

Two horny kids with their fingers on the trigger.

I wasn't a kid anymore.

I was twice this one's age and I wasn't smiling.

It's hard to know what it takes to get one person to kill another. I don't mean the accidental heat-of-the-moment you-bitch-you-bastard bang-you're-dead in the middle of a tiff type killing. I mean the kind when you plan for it, when you think about it, consider it and convince yourself it's a sound idea.

When my father was a ranch hand and they'd gone up to Saskatchewan to bring the cattle down for roundup in the spring, a Mountie appeared out of nowhere. As my father put it in Yiddish, "Cimnt arein a Mountie." He told the foreman he was looking for Mishka Kahana. The foreman pointed to my father.

"Mishka Kahana?" asked the Mountie.

He was a big, nice-looking shaigetz, my father told me. Six one, six two, a baby-faced recruit with apple cheeks and a buzz cut 'do. He rode a chestnut mare.

"I'm supposed to take you in, sir," said the Mountie. "I have instructions to bring you back to appear before a magistrate in Lethbridge."

"Mishka here's an honest man," the foreman told the Mountie.

"I have my instructions," the Mountie told the foreman.

"I've got work," said my father, for whom work was a religion. "What if I said no?"

The Mountie let his hand slide down his side where the gun butt peeked out from underneath the leather flap of his holster and the lanyard fastened to the metal ring and looped back up to his epaulet. The mare snorted steam in the morning cold and her muscles twitched along her foreleg. She stomped at the mud and melted snow.

"I have my instructions. You're to come along with me, Mr. Kahana."

My father looked over to the foreman. He knew of the bad blood between my dad and my uncle. Deportation. It was my uncle's ultimate weapon over his brother and my father never knew if or when he would use it. He knew only that for him deportation meant death. He was after all an enemy of the people, a sinner in the worker's paradise sentenced to die for crimes against the state.

"Better go with him, Mishka," said the foreman. "He's the law."

"Yeah," my father said. "I get my bedroll and my rucksack."

My father got his gear. He slipped the sleeping robe up along the horse's rump and tied it to the saddle with the leather thongs. He tied it slowly and methodically and all the while he watched the Mountie. My father was in his midthirties. He was a man. He had killed men. He had watched them die and lain in ambush waiting to kill them. He had seen them in his sights and it was no game and he squeezed the trigger. He had killed them with a thirty aught six Czech Mauser and with a Browning thirty-caliber machine gun. He had done one with a knife. He was in the First World War and the Russian Revolution, but it was not until the Civil War that followed the Revolution that he learned all there was to know about brutality, he said. He had seen it. He had done some of it. He had done it for causes he no longer believed in. He had done it mainly because he knew if he didn't kill the ones he killed, they would surely have done it to him. So as he tied the old fur sleeping robe onto the saddle, he watched the Mountie and thought, What would be the best way to kill him?

The Mountie took my father's rifle. The Mountie had one of his own as well as his .38 caliber pistol. Where my father was a man, the Mountie still looked very much like a boy. He had the rosy cheeks and tufts of golden fuzz where he'd not shaved. There was a softness to his face. He looked well rested and well fed. He looked like someone loved him. He looked like a nice young man with many plans for a future my father would cut short. My father had no intention of being deported.

He told me later he never considered not killing the Mountie for an instant. He was not even aware that it was a decision that could or could not have been made. It was simply what had to happen. You don't think to make the sun come up, he told me, it just does.

The Mountie was big. He looked strong. The way farm boys look strong. Long and rangy. No fat, just easy muscles, sinew and bone. He moved with a lovely athletic grace and his shiny boots made my father think of a line in an Isaac Babel story. A Jew looks at a Cossack's boots. The calf muscles were curvy as a young girl's bottom, wrapped in shiny leather. Or something like that. My father came from a generation of well-read killers. They knew Tolstoy and Dostoyevsky, Pushkin and Proust. "All the literature," my father said, "all that great writing, beautiful thoughts, beautiful words. Didn't keep one person from being killed. I read everything Tolstoy wrote. It didn't slow me up even for a little bit. It just . . . gave me something to think about. That didn't make the people I killed any the less dead. Nor would it have done me any good if I hadn't shot them first."

"You like Tolstoy, maybe?" my father asked the Mountie.

"The writer, eh?" the Mountie asked my father.

"No, the baker," Mishka said as they rode out of camp across the still-frozen tundra that was melting into mud.

"I don't know any Tolstoy who's a baker."

"Okay, so what about the writer? You know Tolstoy the writer?"

"I've heard his name," the Mountie said, keeping his eyes all the while on my father's hands.

"But you've never read him," said Mishka, watching the young Mountie like a very wise old mongoose.

"No, sir," said the Mountie. "I'm not much for storybooks. I quite fancy the flickers, though. I quite like that little fellow with the glasses who's always getting himself into trouble, hanging off the clock towers and the like."

My father wanted him to talk. If he talked at all he was a fool. But if he talked for any length of time, he'd be a dead fool. He'd show my father how to kill him. He'd show him where he was strong and where soft.

Sure enough it didn't take long. My father decided this was a well-fed farm boy, probably with a nice plump little wife, someone warm to snuggle up to, soft as a quilt and milky-smelling, comfortable. That's what she'd be. Not some hellion you'd stay up all night screwing, but someone soft and warm and comfortable that you'd snuggle in close to and sleep sound as a baby. Little kettzle, my father thought about the Mountie. He's going to get sleepy talking and talking and when he does, I'll crush his skull.

"You got a wife, maybe?" my father asked.

"Yes, I have," said the Mountie.

"Is she your sweetheart, from the school, maybe . . . from the Sunday school could be, huh?"

"Why, yes," said the young officer. "People always said we were like Tom Sawyer and Becky Thatcher."

"You've got a picture?" my father asked.

"Yes," the rosy-cheeked boy answered wistfully. "And of our little one as well."

He reached inside the breast pocket of his tunic and took out a new leather case. A Christmas present. He opened it and there was a picture of the three of them. The rosy-cheeked Mountie and his plump and pretty wife, her breasts heavy from nursing their little baby girl, and the little baby girl, with her father's rosy cheeks and mother's dimples smiled up at my father from the photograph.

They made a small cook fire that night and spread out their bedrolls on oilcloths to keep the damp out. My father asked if the Mountie had any whiskey.

"Just for the chill, you know, it's raw out tonight."

But instead, the Mountie made coffee. So my father drank most of it, thinking, He's got to get sleepy sometime. He's got to nod off. There was a rock the size of a basketball not more than a few feet away. It would have weighed a good fifty pounds. As soon as the Mountie was asleep he'd kill him with it. He'd stand over him, raise the rock above his head, and heave it down hard as he could.

Hard as he could was awfully hard at that. It would be like killing a cow in the slaughterhouse. My father had done that as well, crushed their skulls with sledgehammers, sweated in the hot blood stench of the big slaughter shops, waded in blood and brains, knee deep. A Mountie's skull would be no harder than a cow's, he thought. Killing cows didn't bother him. For that matter, killing men hadn't bothered him much either. There was never a doubt. It was war and they were enemies. The rules of war were simple. Kill them first. My father was a rule follower.

But this was different. There was no war. There were no shellbursts in the skies. Just stars, clear and white-cold like holes punched in black sky that masked a moon hiding out behind it. And he didn't get sleepy either. All he did was talk. He talked about the wife, about the bairn, as he called his daughter, about their plans, about the sweet smell of talcum and the warmth of home and hearth, the comforting smells of his young wife's cooking and the strange way his daughter's cooing almost made him cry. And the more he talked, the less tired he seemed.

"I'm such a lucky man," he said. If he said it once, he said it a dozen times. "I'm such a lucky man."

My father was disgusted, and despite the copious amounts of the Mountie's coffee he had drunk, he was tired, tired of not having all the things the Mountie went home to every night, tired of being a single man living on a cot in a wooden room with other single men farting beneath their blankets in the night.

"You're luckier than you know," my father said, handing the Mountie back the picture of the family my father wished were his own. "Luckier than you know," he said and turned over to go to sleep. He could always kill a border guard.

When they got back to Lethbridge, they rode up to the new brick courthouse and hitched their horses next to a Model T. The Mountie got down and stood next to my father with his stupid farm boy baby fat look.

What a puppy, my father thought. What a kitten. Little kettzle. "Okay," he said. "Let's go."

"Mr. Kahana," said the Mountie.

"What?" answered my father.

"I do not know if you could have done what you were thinking of doing out there the other night," he said, looking my father in the eye with a look that seemed much older than his years. "But I very much appreciate the fact that you didn't try, sir."

My father looked him up and down. "Thank

your little daughter," said my father. "The little kettzle . . ."

"You're a decent man, Mr. Kahana," said the Mountie. "I do not know what you are wanted for, but if it will help, I'll be happy to tell the magistrate what I know of your decency."

They walked together into the courthouse, the Mountie who was bringing my father to his death and my father who had let the Mountie live because of a photograph of a dimpled baby girl with her father's rosy cheeks. They stood before the magistrate, who thanked the Mountie for bringing Mr. Kahana so he could be sworn in as a subject of His Majesty and a citizen of the British Commonwealth of Nations and of Canada, which was now his country and from which he never need fear deportation again.

"They didn't tell the poor schmuck what he had to bring me in for. It was to give me citizenship, and I could have killed him, could have crushed his skull. So what stopped it in the end? Tolstoy? Dostoyevsky? Pushkin? No. God made him show me the picture."

So that night, my father told me, God did three things. He saved the Mountie's life. He enabled my father to become a citizen, and He convinced him that it was time to get married and start a family of his own. Shortly thereafter he asked a friend where the best-looking women in North America were. Then he started saving money and when his savings reached three thousand dollars, he left the wilds of Canada and came down to Long Beach and met my mother.

Consider then my position. Not on the frozen tundra of the Alberta outback, but the loamy soil and humid nights of Wailea, watching not a rosy-cheeked Mountie with a photo of his plump and pretty bride and newborn child, but a sallow-cheeked wastrel shtupping the shit out of Nora Wolfe, the woman who had approached me first, after all, to kill her husband. And if I'd only taken her up on that I wouldn't be out here swatting sand fleas right now, watching them do the big nasty through the plantation shutters. So what was there to reprieve Chad? Western literature was not the ticket, and if the man possessed the photo of a baby, it had probably come along with a letter that said, "It's yours, you scum-sucking sack of shit, you owe money," and it would've been signed Heidi or Brandee or Tawny. So no cigar there, either, since he wouldn't have paid, and Tawny, Heidi, or Brandee would be only too happy to read his obituary.

It had not dawned on me until that moment that I was perhaps in a dysfunctional relationship. Worse still, was the fact that however dysfunctional the relationship was, it was one-sided as well. A voyeur, one could only suppose, could not rightfully claim to be in a relationship with the voyee. Which of course makes the whole thing all the more frustrating.

The only thing, in fact, that kept me from

killing him, that kept me from sneaking up behind him and putting a bullet through his brain or sneaking up towards him and shooting his nuts off and then double-tapping him between the eyes was Joan Chan.

Not to say that Joan Can talked me out of it. It's just that I knew that if I killed Chad, no matter how smart I played it, no matter how I covered my tracks or made it look like a drug deal gone south, Detective Chan would figure it out and nail my ass to the wall. The truth was, I did not let Chad live because of my compassion or morality. I did it simply because I knew without the shadow of a doubt that Joan Chan was smarter than I.

She would be on it like a bloodhound, like soy on rice. She would sink her teeth into it and not let go until she had busted the most publicized case on the island. "Haole Jew cop kills paramour's lover in midshtup."

I went out and got completely shitfaced and in that alkie logic, I considered for a time that perhaps the thing to do was kill Joan Chan. No one was as smart as her. With her out of the way everybody was just as dumb as me. I had a fifty-fifty shot. But then I remembered that Joan Chan was not only smarter but a better marksman, so I busted little Chaddie instead.

I surveilled the little shit till I saw him selling hemp to a local surfer. I badged him and drew down like he was Jeffrey Dahmer or something. I patted him down and then turned him around and said, "Hit me."

"What?" he said.

"Hit me," I bellowed like De Niro in *Raging Bull.*

"Whoa," he said in his best pre-*Speed* Keanu Reeves. "This is bullshit, dude."

"Hit me, you piece of shit."

"I'm not gonna hit you, man," he said. Then he looked at me more closely. "Whoa, shit. I, like, know who you are now, man. You're, like, that old guy Nora used to ball."

That's when I hit him. I caught him with a hard right into his eye. I kicked him in the nuts, grabbed him by the ears, and slammed his head down into my fast-rising knee. That's when he threw his shoulder into my gut and jammed me back against the wall. For a degenerate he was a very strong kid. Thank God for pepper spray.

"This is bullshit bust, you know that, don't you Kahana?"

It was the Major. "You lost the evidence. You didn't Mirandize him and everybody on the island knows this is the kid that was slammin' his bambucha to Nora Wolfe, that Haole lady with the slit dress."

I blinked at the Major. "How the fuck did . . . Major, honest to God, I swear . . ." I said. "I mean what's this deal about Nora Wolfe? That's bullshit. Is that what that kid said? Are you gonna take his word over mine, sir?"

"No," said the Major. "I'm going to take Joan Chan's word over yours."

I caught up with Joan Chan in the Day Room.

"You're supposed to be my partner," I said. "Where do you get off, A, screwing up a righteous bust, and B, telling the Major that I got this kid out of jealousy? What the fuck are you trying to do to me, huh, Joan?"

"A, it wasn't a righteous bust and you know it," said Joan Chan. "And B, you bust this kid and at the trial they'll get ten people to swear the only reason you did it was because he was sticking the pork sword to your former tootsie, about whom you are still evidently as they say in pidgin, hu-hu."

"Who's hu-hu?"

"You's hu-hu," said Joan Chan, "about Nora Wolfe, and everybody knows it."

"What are you talking about everybody knows it," I said in the same anguish I had felt living on the kibbutz in Israel, where everyone knew what color underwear you were wearing on what day. "How the hell does anybody know anything?"

"It's an *iiiisland*," Joan Chan said. "It's small, that's why they call it an island, because everybody knows what everybody else is doing."

Later in the afternoon I ran into Schvester Rochelle. Sister One was over from Honolulu to help set up a chaplaincy program for Maui County.

"Would you like to talk to me about something, my son? Do you feel the need to be in counseling?"

Sister Rochelle said in her best Pat O'Brien brogue.

"Counseling about what, Schvester?"

"Counseling about why you're such a schmuck," Sister Rochelle said and punched me in the bicep. "Cops cannot use their police powers to eliminate rivals who are twenty years younger. It's bad form and it can get you thrown off the force or into jail."

"Jesus," I said. "Is there anybody on this island who *doesn't* know about my personal life?"

"No," said Sister One, and then she fixed me with those cold nun eyes of hers, "there isn't. And everybody knows that but you."

"All right, all right," I said. "I'll drop the charges against the kid. Fine."

"Did it ever occur to you," said Sister Rochelle, "that since everyone on the island *does* know about you and Nora and Nora and this boy, that maybe you were being used?"

"What's that mean?" I asked.

"It means you're a jealous person, Denil, and jealous people can always be used for something."

Five

"Jesus, Lovey," said Jack Wolfe. "Nice thinking. Lovely touch. It's why I love you, you
know, even though you can't stand me, and don't
think that doesn't hurt or at least cause some very
real anguish, because it does . . . but anyway, nice
thinking. I love that mind of yours . . . almost as
much as I love that sweet little ass and those—"

"Shut up, Jack," Nora Wolfe said to her husband as she poured a double Absolut into a glass,
dropped in ice, a drop of vermouth, and a twist.
She crossed out of the white room onto the lanai
overlooking Wailea Point and the seven caves
where the sharks slept till they came up to feed.

"See, that's what I mean about the hurt part,
Lovey," Jack said, coming up behind her and slip-

ping his hand up her thigh onto her stomach. "I talk about your sweet ass and your wonderful mind and you say, shut up. It's real anguish for me. But it was a lovely touch about the boy and your kosher cop friend. How did you know he was watching you? Why do I ask? Of course you knew. You get off on it. Show time, huh, Lovey?" he said and stuck his finger in her drink and then into his mouth. "Uch, vermouth," he said. "Mosquito piss."

Jack Wolfe hated vermouth. But nothing could dampen his mood. His eyes closed halfway, down to slits so he could see nothing but a horizontal cut of coastline.

He always told her the big picture was not what would trip you up. It was the narrow picture, the small details that could make or break you.

"Lovely detail," he said in the tone of voice he reserved for talking about fourteen-year-old dark-skinned girls in Mozambique. "Lovely detail. Our gun-toting Yid watches the lithe boy and you making the beast with two backs. He hates the boy now worse than me, so that when I turn up dead . . . well I'm not saying there'll be any pity for poor old Jack, but still, he'll pursue my killer with real gusto I think, don't you, Lovey? And he certainly won't want to see you go to prison. He'll probably even fantasize that with poor old Jack and the boy toy both out of the way, maybe you and he could . . . what? Spend shabbas together or something, eh, Lovey? Pesach in Poipu. I'm being too ethnic for you I know, Lovey, aren't I?"

By that time Nora has already stepped off the lanai and down to her car.

"Where are you going, Lovey?" Jack called out.

"I'm going to see Chad."

"Okay," said Jack Wolfe, waving to her with his fingertips. "Have a good time. Don't forget to make sure he uses protection."

He picked up her glass and raised it to her car as it tore out of the drive. "Chin-chin," he said and took a sip and then made a face. "Uch," he said. "Vermouth."

"Idiot!" she yelled and then slapped him. She caught him hard across his cheek and the corner of his mouth, slammed a bit of lip into a crooked canine tooth that all the local girls thought made this Haole boy look so sexy.

"Whoa, shit," he said, and put his hand up to his cheek where the red imprint of Nora's palm had started to glow. He brought his hand down and saw the blood and licked at it. "Shit."

"He's watching you now," she said and pulled out a cigarette, flicked her lighter once and again and again, heard no hiss of gas so looked around Chad's grubby apartment for a match. There were overturned beer cans and roaches, the ones that crawled and the ones you smoked. There was moldy yogurt and rotten fruit that smelled sickly sweet, like a disease. There were underwear and socks behind the bathroom door, peeking out beneath the cracked and peeling paint of the bathroom door that never shut all the way because the knob was permanently loose.

"What a hovel," she said and rubbed her thumb against her forefinger, feeling the dust and grease she had just rubbed off the countertop like a sergeant major inspecting the barracks.

"Who's watching me?" Chad asked as he moved toward the mirror to look at his lip. His eye was still swollen red and purple. My ring marks were still evident on both sides of his jaw.

"Kahana," Nora said and crossed across his floor like Indiana Jones picking his way through a booby-trapped ruin as she stepped over a broken beer mug here, a mildewed apple core there, until she stood before his stove, lit a burner, held her hair back against her neck, and bent over the blue flame and sucked it into her cigarette.

"That cop?" Chad said and dabbed at his lip with his dish towel, leaving bloodstains there to join the others. "He dropped the charges."

Nora started to lean back against the counter and then remembered the grease on her fingertips so stood erect, smoking. "I'm not talking about some stupid little drug bust, Chad."

"Hey," said Chad with a wounded look. "Don't call me stupid."

Amazing, she thought looking at him, he takes offense to that.

"Chad," she said crossing to him, reaching up with one hand and down with the other, kissing him where he bled. "Listen to me. It's very important that you listen to me and focus on exactly what I'm saying, okay?"

"What?" he said, sulking.

"Don't sulk. This is business now. We can't afford the luxury of sulking, you understand? So listen to me openly and objectively, with a focused mind and a serious intent. A deadly serious intent. Not only our lives depend on that, but a great deal of money as well. All right?"

She kissed him, pushed up against him, felt him rise against her stomach, and saw him smile his cocky I'm-gonna-get-laid-now-oh-boy smile.

"Okay," he said.

"You have a beautiful body," she said in a calm voice as if listing the attributes of a piece of real estate.

"Oh, baby, so do you. You got a dynamite bod," Chad said and pulled her in closer.

Nora pushed him back a bit, the way you'd discipline a stupid dog.

"I need you to listen," she said firmly. "You have a beautiful body and you're very athletic with it in bed. You have wonderful skin and gorgeous eyes and hair that most women would kill for."

Chad was starting to smile now in spite of himself.

"But," Nora said, "you *are* very stupid."

"Hey," said Chad, jutting his chin and stepping back from her.

"That doesn't mean," Nora continued in a calm

soothing voice, "that you can't have me or that we can't kill Jack and get all of his money *and* get away with it. That doesn't mean that we can't get everything we want. It *does* mean however that we have to be very, very smart, because Jack is very, very smart, and Jack knows that we are going to try and kill him."

"He does?" yelped Chad, involuntarily, almost in pain. "How does he know? How the fuck does he know?"

"Please, Chad," Nora said, sucking the last little bit of her cigarette. "Jack is smart."

"So you don't, like, know he knows, huh?" said Chad hopefully.

It was incredible. Chad was so gorgeous and yet at moments like these he could make her appreciate Jack.

"Look," she said. "Jack tells me go out and find a pretty boy, seduce him, and we'll make it look like he killed the husband in order to have the horny wife all to himself. Then he offers to split his own insurance money with me, and he does this at a time when I'm *already* sleeping with you. *Of course* he knows that you and I will try to *really* kill him. That's why we've got to be smarter than him."

That's when it hit Chad, penetrated the haze of drugs and sex and sun and ego that was his life. Jack knew. She knew he knew. He knew she knew he knew. It was a game they were playing. The ultimate S & M trip. Try and kill me though I'm watching, and let me watch while you do it. And for her it was the rush, the excitement, the real high of it all, knowing he *was* watching. It was just like the way she walked down the street . . . goin' do wah ditty ditty dum ditty do.

"So, Lovey," Jack said when she got back the next morning, "Have a good time? Listen, of course you did. I can see it by the glow. It's good for you, this young stallion, eh? You know what I wish?"

"What?" Nora said, slipping out of her clothes and into her shower as Jack watched.

"I don't know," Jack said. "Call me sentimental you know, but sometimes I wish we could just turn back the clock and have things be like they used to be in the beginning between us, when you'd fuck those business people and then tell me about it and we'd get each other off."

"You want me to tell you what it's like to be with him, Jack?" Nora asked over the sound of the water.

"Only if you like," he said. "I don't want to pry."

"What a freak," she said softly.

"That's us, Lovey. It's why we worked so well together, you know?"

So she told him as she showered and he watched her through the glass and rubbed himself as he listened and watched. And she saw him and knew that it was working. In spite of himself, she could still capture him for a moment, hold him there and get his mind off trying to figure out how she intended to murder him.

"So, Lovey," Jack said later, after she had finally gotten up from the Seconal snooze, "shall we sit around the old kitchen table and plan how to murder me?"

"Sure," said Nora.

She was wearing a white silk kimono that fell open down to the belt at her waist and made her look even more tan than she was.

He sat across from her and poured a small tumbler of Pernod. "Vodka?" he asked.

"Please," she said.

He poured her Absolut and the hint of vermouth. He knew exactly the right amount. No one did it better. The ice was right, the twist was right. There was no bite. Just cold fire.

"Nothin' says lovin', eh, Lovey?" he said as he handed her the drink.

She took a little sip.

"You're a degenerate," she said, "but you do make a killer martini."

"Je vous en pris," he said with a sickeningly modest bow. "So, speaking of killing, what do you think would be the best way of murdering me?"

"Preferably something that involves pain," she said, taking another sip and smiling.

"That goes without saying," he said and sipped at his Pernod. "It should be something that at first blush appears to be an accident. Poor Jack should be killed in an accident. You, the grieving widow, go to the insurance company, and now—thanks to you and that lovely touch with Kahana—there will be an immediate suspicion on his part. No. More than suspicion. Before you aroused his jealousy I would say suspicion was the most we could have gotten, but now he is going to positively *hope* that it was murder and not an accident. We can depend on a most rigorous investigation. So here is my approach. First I have to think to myself, how would I actually murder poor old Jack, if that was in fact my goal. If I was beautiful and pushing forty and had a sweet ass like yours and the young stallion going bumpson with me. By the way, have you ever thought of such a thing, Lovey, of how you would *actually* murder me?"

"All the time. With gusto," Nora said. "I'd do it slowly."

"Ohhhh, you sexy bitch," he said. "But really, Lovey. It must have two elements. First, it must succeed and second I mustn't get caught. This isn't just pleasure, after all. It's business. Right?"

"Right as rain," she said.

"So I look up the actuarial tables from the insurance companies and I think to myself, what is it that is an established part of my life that provides the greatest possibility for accidental death, outside of being married to an energetic young woman with an insatiable sexual appetite of course. And you know what I find?"

She was listening intently now and it was a mark of the depth of her own greed that she did not allow her hatred for her husband to in any way alter or diminish her appreciation for his cunning. In that regard, she admired him above all other men.

"I find my beloved boat. There's an advantage, Lovey, in having an old boat, just as there is in having an older lover, eh? First, of course, the subtlety of lines, the character that only wood can convey instead of these fiberglass monstrosities, but for our purposes the real advantage is the danger. You see, in an old boat you must turn on the blower before you start the engine. It's because gas fumes collect under the deck in the dark hole where the vessel's throbbing power plant lies dormant until the spark from the ignition brings it roaring to life. So there, under the deck in this enclosed space, you have . . . what? Gas fumes. An enclosed space, and a spark. Hence the rule about the blower. But if the blower isn't working properly, or if the little vents are clogged, instead of the engine throbbing with power, thrusting its pistons in and out, in and out, you have what?"

"A bomb," she said, leaning toward him, the kimono opening just a bit.

"A very big bomb. Very deadly and very thorough. There would hardly be a body part left to identify."

So they sat there, the two of them, at the kitchen table drinking their vodka and Pernod, plotting murder. So many details. So many loose little things to be identified, catalogued, tagged. So many problems begging solutions. A bomb was nice, yes, that's true. An explosion addressed so many concerns. It called attention to itself without question. It fixed the time of death. It involved not only life insurance, but as an added bonus, insurance on the vessel itself. But then the questions. Where indeed *are* the body parts? One could accept the fact that a boat which turned suddenly into a fiery ball of death could devour most of its victim, but even that fiery monster would have to spit out a bone here or there. Surely a piece of flesh might get caught between death's teeth to be flossed out at some point in time and leave enough forensics to allow for identification of the body. If there were insufficient body parts, would not someone smell a rat?

"Lovey, honestly, it's so wonderful to have someone to share this burden with. You're such a good partner. You ask all the questions just like the cops. But see this is why I'm thinking of the boat, you see. It's just like Greta Kraft, you remember, that society bitch with the young gigolo who fed her to the sharks and then married the hula dancer? The one who was shtupping the movie star? What did they find of her? You know, it was a fibia or tibia or . . . a wishbone or something. But it wasn't much. That's really the beauty of a killing at sea. You have all these sharks and they're so hungry and there are so many of them and they eat and eat and eat . . . with those big crooked teeth. You know, so what's going to be left? An olive pit maybe."

He sat back and looked out past her through the sliding doors that gave off the kitchen to the lanai, where a moon hung like a blood orange over the bay, reflecting phosphorus plankton that shone red with every crest of wave that hit the shore.

"I mean, I'm not going to cut off an arm or leg for this thing."

They both sat there thinking.

"If Lorena Bobbitt snipped Mister Happy on a boat and tossed it overboard, they wouldn't have found a thing. So I don't see why we have to be holier than the Pope about this. So they don't find a body part. It was an explosion for goodness sake. It blows the body up into little bitsy pieces and then the sharks come and eat them. We anchor at La Parouse. There are currents aren't there? The Alenuihaha Channel? So maybe little pieces of poor old Jack are washing up in Fiji or Tarowa or whatever that island is where the natives screw each other all day long."

"Your teeth," Nora said, tapping the enamel of her own beautiful smile.

"What about them?" Jack said, leaning back away from her protectively.

"We pull a few," Nora said, grinning now.

"Don't you have some teeth that were capped in Shanghai during the war?"

"Well, I don't think we need to . . ."

For the first time in a long time Nora was having fun. Not the kind of fun she usually thought of, which was drug-induced or involved orgasm. Rather, this was what people once called good clean fun, the kind other people might experience from having just laid out a fourteen-letter word with triple bonus points in Scrabble. Only in her case, it centered around the fact that she had just come up with the idea of pulling a molar or two out of her husband's jaw in order to fake his murder so that the two of them could split his insurance. The bonus points part in this instance came, of course, from the fact that his murder would not be faked at all. He'd go through the pain of having his teeth pulled *and* be killed as well, while she split the money with her fifteen-years-younger lover. So this was fun.

He had to admit that it was a great idea. He indeed had teeth which had been capped in Shanghai during the war. The caps were distinctive, and here in the islands with their large Chinese population there was probably a dentist or two who could identify the work.

Nora volunteered to pull them herself.

"No thank you, Lovey," Jack said. He wanted it done with anesthetic.

"You never let me have any fun," Nora said, feigning a pout.

Then she feigned sincerity.

"But really, Jack," she said. "You certainly can't go to a dentist and have the teeth pulled, because then he could testify against us. I'm only thinking of the good of the plan."

"You're a saint, Lovey," Jack said. "An honest to God saint. No, I can find an old Chinaman who can pull it. Some old herbalist who can give me maybe some opium and will keep his mouth shut.

It certainly was true that there were ancient Chinese in the Islands who neither spoke nor read any English at all and for whom the goings-on of the white world might as well be happening on the dark side of the moon. Such an old medicine man would never hear, much less care about the death of a German Jewish Haole transplant. And if questioned by the police, such elderly Celestials became positively Sphinx-like.

They talked about salting the bottom depths beneath the boat with a few planks splattered with Jack's own blood on the off chance that some of the DNA might still be identifiable. Nora thought Jack ought to be willing to cut off a finger as well. Not a thumb mind you. But just a digit. They were after all talking about a great deal of money. Jack ought to be willing to sacrifice something.

For his part he argued that he had already agreed to have teeth extracted which would then be planted on the sandy ocean floor.

"Teeth shmeeth," Nora said, slightly drunk after three hours of vodka-laced plotting. "What about your ring finger. How's that? Huh? Your ring finger, with your wedding ring still on it so they really have something to identify then. I mean, they can show me your finger in a little box or something."

"I think they put them in baggies," said Jack. "You know . . . the Ziploc kind. I don't think they put them in a box."

"Okay, so they'll show me a baggie, Jack. What's the big deal? They show me a baggie with your finger in it and I can hold it up and . . ."

Here it was truly impressive. Even drunk, or perhaps because she was drunk, Nora was able to conjure up real tears, to quiver her lip and send ripples through the tiny muscles across her chin.

"Oh my God," she said, fighting back the tears. "That's the ring I gave him. That's Jack's wedding ring." And then she cried. Then she looked up, dry-eyed.

"That's very effective, Jack," she said evenly. "A finger with the wedding ring still on it is very, very effective. I don't know how they'd be able to argue about that."

"No!" said Jack, shrinking back from her almost in physical pain, almost feeling the bone crushed beneath the blade.

"You're so close-minded," Nora said and the tone of almost affection which had been there only a moment before completely vanished.

"Now, Lovey," said Jack.

"Don't say, now, Lovey to me, Jack," said Nora,

mimicking her husband's accent. "It's just because it's my idea. If you'd thought it up, you'd think it was wonderful."

"Honestly, Lovey, if I'd thought it up I'd think it was stupid too."

"It's not stupid," Nora said. "It's irrefutable proof that you're dead."

"No, it isn't."

"Yes, it is," she said and lit a cigarette.

"No, it isn't. They look at the finger. They see it's been cut off with a knife. They can tell those sorts of things, Lovey. You know they're very scientific. So then they know it wasn't from an explosion and it wasn't from any shark unless you want to tell me he was dining with a full set of cutlery."

"We could cut it off with a serrated edge," Nora insisted, "Or we could cut it off with a straight edge but cut it off high . . . right up to the knuckle and then we could buy a set of real shark's teeth at one of those souvenir shops on Front Street and we could put the teeth on it and take a hammer and pound right through so we'd have a real shark bite," she said. "I mean the truth is, Jack, there are any number of things we could do if you really cared. I mean if you cared more about making this perfect than you did about protecting your ego."

"I'm not protecting my ego," Jack said defensively. "I'm protecting my finger."

"Oh no," said Nora with disgust. "This isn't about fingers. This is about ego. Just like always."

The two of them were silent after a while, filled with icy stares out to sea, Jack said, "You know, Lovey, I was really enjoying this for a while. I mean it was so nice just to sit here you know, like an old married couple, making plans together, and then you have to go and spoil it. Honestly, I had such warm feelings toward you."

But the feelings were gone. They were tied together only by their business now. And their business was murder.

It was not long thereafter on one of the days when Nora fled Maui for her hairdresser in Honolulu, when Chad was coming out of the water near the place he called Two Heads Point because of the two portable toilets which had been set up there for road crews the year before when he had found the place quite by accident, where the waves were close to perfect every day for about an hour in the late afternoon, that he heard a voice which quite literally sent shivers more violent than any caused by the cold air of the late afternoon wind that whipped the foam up off the tops of the waves.

It was Jack's voice. He stood behind Chad as Chad was toweling off. He had a gun in his hand and he was smiling as he said, "Hello, Chad, I think we need to talk."

Six

"Hello, Chad, I think we need to talk."

Those were the words, but they meant nothing to Chad. They certainly didn't mean what the words "Hello, Chad, I think we need to talk" are normally meant to convey.

"Hello, Chad, I think we need to talk" were the words a principal said, or a vice principal, a guidance counselor, or a cop.

"Hello Chad, I think we need to talk" were the words a lover said. Well, let's call it what it is without granting it any undue dignity. "Hello, Chad, I think we need to talk" were the words a girlfriend, a tootsie, a main or minor squeeze, might use. She might say, "Hello Chad, I think we need to talk. This relationship is going nowhere. I know what I want in life. I want to get married. I want to have children and it's clear that you lack that kind of commitment." So the talk in question is one which might cost a little emotional pain, but if indeed the pain were too great, the antidote would be simple. All one might need to do in such circumstances would be to say, Okay, let's get married. Let's have children and grow old and wrinkled together. Until one day you take my wizened hand in your liver-spotted arthritic one and we make our suicide pact or you put me in the home with some West Indian woman who will beat me when you're gone unless our children care enough to buy a surveillance camera.

Either way, it won't matter to me because I'll be senile but at least we will have gotten there together. Is that not the mark of a successful relationship? The long, slow walk toward senility, insolvency, incontinence? But wait. Perhaps I'm getting just a tad ahead of myself. We were after all talking about the words "Hello, Chad, I think we need to talk."

Taken another way, they could simply mean, "I'm pregnant." As in, "Hello Chad, I think we need to talk . . . I'm pregnant." Well, at any rate that was the great fear of my youth. The "I think we need to talk" part was followed always by "I'm late," as in "I'm pregnant." I had a friend some people thought of as heartless who upon hearing those words "I'm pregnant," said, "Drink lots of milk." Others, like me for instance, said things that meant, "I'll stand by you. Have the baby. I'll be your husband" or "Don't have the baby, I'll pay for the abortion."

Perhaps the nightmare sentence today that follows the uttered musing that perhaps there is need for a conversation is along the lines of "I'm positive," as in "I tested positive," as in "I'm HIV positive," as in "You're going to die, you putz, for a one-night stand and a quick dip of the proverbial wick. Your ass is dead." Be that as it may, it is not an immediate death. I'm not saying it's not a painful one, a debilitating one, a death worthy of marches, vigils, and ribbons, indeed jewelry in the shape of ribbons, but it is nonetheless not a bang-you're-dead death.

This, on the other hand, was.

This was "Chad, we need to talk because I'm about to blow your fucking brains out."

That was at any rate how Chad perceived it.

This after all was the husband of the woman he was energetically shtupping who had said to the woman, "Find a boy whom we can frame for my death and then we'll split the insurance," which woman had told the boy, "Let's not fake it but *really* kill him and *we'll* split the insurance," who had then later told the boy that they had to be careful because the aforementioned husband most certainly *knew* that that self-same woman had not only found a boy but *told* the boy all the plans, including kill him and then *we'll* split the insurance, which freely translated into "He *knew* that they *knew* that he *knew*" and the "he" in question was now standing in front of Chad at Two Heads Point with what appeared to be a cocked and loaded thirty-eight caliber automatic and he was saying to that boy who was so central to both the woman and the man's plans for deception and for murder, "Hello, Chad, I think we need to talk."

Chad wanted nothing more at that moment than to crawl back inside his mother's womb, which leads me inexorably to this meditation: The bond between parent and child is perhaps the most powerful one in the entire realm of human experience.

Consider this par example: Upon hearing and indeed seeing proof of the red-cheeked Mountie's love for his child, my own father decided

A) not to kill the Mountie, and
B) to get him some kids of his own.

If that is not proof enough, consider then, devoted reader, that Schvester Rochelle, Sister Rachel, Sister One herself on the night she and I got shitfaced after Captain Jarhead failed to make good on his pronounced intentions of sending her to Jesus, that self-same Sister One in the throes of Old Bushmills–induced intoxication confessed to me, a Jew no less, that perhaps she had royally fucked up in becoming a nun and marrying a non-corporal deity, to wit, Jesus, and should instead have married Clarence Murphy O'Brien, her child-hood love who now had three daughters, nine grandchildren, and two great-grandchildren.

Clarence Murphy O'Brien was not the cause of her alcohol-induced and confessed regret, it was the daughters, and their children and children's children.

"I wish, sometimes," she said, "I had a daughter," and the tears rolled down her cheeks. "When he was pointing that gun at me tonight and I knew honestly, Denil, I knew, in my heart and soul, mind you, that I was going to die, right there, tonight, die and meet my maker, I thought, dear God, why did I not have children? Why didn't I have a daughter? Oh, Denil, it's what I always wanted, you know, to be a mother, to have a little girl, a little baby girl, a daughter, and here I was with that red-necked oaf pointing his gun at me and it wasn't really the thought that I was going to die that got to me so much. It was the true and certain knowledge that die or not, tonight or the next night, or the next one after that, I would die barren, no daughter, no granddaughter, no little baby who called me Mum, no one who would miss me but some other old and barren, hairy-cheeked nun."

"I'd miss you, Schvester," I said, belching bourbon.

"You don't count," she said. "You're nothing but a drunken cop."

"Listen to me, Schvester, I know what you mean, okay, I know . . ."

"No, you don't," she said shaking her head and then propping it up on her palm.

"Yes, I do," I said.

And the truth was, like my father before me, I did. I too had known a morning when I was going to die. It was during the Yom Kippur War in that space between the cease-fires when one broke down to be replaced by another and that one broke down too. I had been in the army for only ten days.

We still had not been issued dog tags. I was still in jeans and tennis shoes and the long-awaited fatigues and combat boots had yet to make their appearance. Everything had been sent to the front, and then we were sent to the front too. We were there to be what they called a presence, to load trucks and ship supplies and man a post taken by the real fighters, so the real fighters could leapfrog forward once again. We were garrison troops. Jobniks they called us, future barbers or supply clerks perhaps, but not fighters. Then, that night, our platoon sergeant, who was a paratrooper, a ruined one, wounded and busted up but a warrior nonetheless, and to us a god, came in and said, "How many here are sole surviving sons?"

Hands went up.

"Gather up your gear," he said. "You're being evacuated."

They're being evacuated, we thought? They're being evacuated? Why the fuck are *they* being evacuated? What is going on here?

The "what is going on here" was a rule in the Israeli Army that sole surviving sons could not serve in combat. We watched as they loaded their kit bags up onto a tender and drove off without us.

Then our platoon sergeant told us.

There was an Iraqi brigade. It was nearby. It would attack at sunup in order to break the cease-fire and force the war to go on, possibly opening a third front with the Jordanians.

Reinforcements could not be moved up because it might appear on satellite photographs to the Americans that we were provoking an attack.

Therefore, they would have to make do with the only troops in that sector. We were the only troops in that sector. Our job, we were told, was to take as long dying as possible. We had to hold out for two hours. That was the amount of time it would probably take to get *real* soldiers up to our position. Someone raised his hand.

"What?" the platoon sergeant asked.

"We don't have any dog tags," someone said.

The platoon sergeant looked at him. "Take a piece of cardboard, and write your name on it," he said. "Put it on a boot lace and then put it around your neck and pray to God you don't burn to death so there'll be something left for your mother to identify."

We were going to die.

Funny the things you'll kill for. Funnier still the things you'll allow your own people to be killed for. Less than a week into the war we were out of everything. A third of the air force was blown away in the first three days. There were stories of pilots attacking the bridges the Egyptians had thrown up across the Suez Canal. So many had been shot down before they could hit their targets that supposedly others had dive-bombed kamikazi-style straight into the bridges, sacrificing their lives to break the link to Egypt.

Schmucks.

They were pontoon bridges. You destroyed one link and in half a day it was repaired.

As far as I know, the pilots were dead forever.

So within a week, we were no longer the military wonder kids of the Middle East. We were shnorrers, dependent on Golda's ability to convince Nixon to send us what we didn't have. Not just bullets and bombs, but shoes, pants, jackets, replacement parts and assault rifles. The Egyptians had been extraordinarily successful in their use of personal antitank weapons. Whole brigades had been decimated by wire-controlled missiles that streaked out of the sands, shattered armor and turned flesh to phosphorus. Now we had not only to regroup and win a military battle, but in order to do that, we had to dance to whatever tune Kissinger played in order to maintain the flow of supplies, the transfusion that could come only from America.

It gave Kissinger the leverage he needed to put geopolitical theories into play and it was paid for, drop by precious drop, with the blood of my friends. Thus, even though intelligence reports indicated beyond a doubt that we would be attacked the next morning, the government had decided that in the larger scheme of things it was more prudent to sacrifice one battalion of freshly minted jobniks than to risk Kissinger's displeasure and the attendant crimp in the IV that stretched from Pennsylvania Avenue to the Ramat David Air Base in Northern Israel.

Better to let them kill us than to endanger the supply lines.

Better by far to make sure they saw us as the victim of attack by not reinforcing our position with *real* soldiers than to have it appear on satellite photographs as if we were provoking an attack.

This was explained to us by our battalion commander, a huge bear of a man whose nickname was Doobo, which meant bear. We had, he said, a right to know why we would die, for what, and what it was worth. It was worth, he said, the survival of the State and our job would be to take as long dying as possible.

But at least two hours.

His words were delivered calmly and quietly and they all made sense. There were some guys who hid under beds, there were even one or two whose bowels opened uncontrollably, but for the most part for all of us that night, we were at peace with ourselves as we loaded clips, cleaned weapons, unpacked brand new ones, wiped away the thick oil coatings and got them ready for combat, and unpacked the new LOW rockets, the one-shot disposable tubes that looked like the kind rolled posters came in.

You pulled a pin, cocked it by pulling the tube apart and the sights popped up. It looked like a cheap toy, but placed well it could stop a tank.

Doobo and his three company commanders poured over marksmanship scores. My father had taught me how to shoot on the ranch.

I had scored well and so would have the privilege of being in one of the lead tank hunter groups.

Everything in the Israeli Army boiled down to groups of threes. Three soldiers was the lowest common denominator. You lived in threes and you died three at a time.

We used a dummy LOW to get used to the sights. We took as many live ones as we could carry. Doobo gathered the tank hunters and said, "You'll get a shot off and then they'll bracket you and you'll be killed. So you have to move as soon as you shoot. You'll have your positions prepared. If they see you move they'll kill you. If they don't, you may get a second or third rocket launched before they find you. I won't lie to you . . . I think it's only a question of how many bonfires you light before they kill you. Be strong and of good courage."

That's how the words translate from the Hebrew. We formed up and moved out. There was no moon and that was in our favor. We got to a jump-off point, then hiked up to a rise about six or eight kilometers farther ahead. We dug in quietly, no smoking, no sounds, not even whispers, knees knocking, bladder bulging, head screaming in pain, trying to camouflage a blind and then a fallback position, trying to figure out how to leapfrog from one to another until they killed us.

Pray to God you don't burn to death, so there'll be something for your mother to identify.

We lay there on the rise on beds of thorn bushes and thistles in holes dug in rocky soil and now and again a whiff of sound would drift up to us, a hiss of Arabic, the glow of a cigarette butt launched into the air from fingers flicking it into the darkness.

Then, before the dawn, before the hint of light, the smell of coffee and tobacco floated up towards us from the Iraqis and then the light.

The attack would come we knew, with the sun in our eyes, from the east. And in the half light, the deep blue dawn light streaked red that bled into the clouds, we saw the camouflage nets come off the turrets, heard the metal scrapings of hatches opening and the muffled clang of iron closings, of men, machines, shells loading, locking down, coiled, ready to spring, the minute they move, we fire. And it never happened.

They stayed there.

We stayed there.

They didn't move.

We didn't breathe.

They didn't move for hours. And then they left. Pulled back. Vanished down behind a hill leaving smells of coffee, cigarettes, diesel, and urine mingling in the air, hanging there behind them. No one died that morning, no flesh burned or was ripped apart by screaming metal hurling through the air to be stopped, dulled, blunted for a moment by bodies and blood.

No one died.

Then we were pulled back too, and left our own smells there for hyenas to sniff at among the rocks and thornbushes. Later it was announced. The new cease-fire. The one that held. And the war was over.

I did not know what happened that night or that morning, why they had left, why no shots were fired, why and for what reason I was still alive and the people I would have killed, why they lived on as well.

Then Kissinger published his memoirs, and on that night while we cleaned weapons, loaded bullets into clips, popped sights on dummy LOWS, dug in, and prepared to kill and die, Kissinger, it seems, had said to Sadat that Golda had gone as far as she could, that the cease-fire now must either be reinstated and held, or the war would go on. If it did, the Israelis would win. The Egyptians would lose what territory they had gained and Kissinger would be left without the lever he would need to put theory into effect and change history. He explained it all to Sadat, what he could win and what he could lose, just as Doobo had explained to us why we would die. And Sadat did the one thing Kissinger had not expected. Instead of saying, Let me think it over, let me talk to my aides, let me confer with my allies, let me sleep on it, read an entrail or two, consult tea leaves or stars, instead of any of that, he said, Tell the old lady she has a deal.

The cease-fire went into effect, held, and on that morning no one died. Not even me.

I decided to get married. I wanted children. I made a list in my mind of every girl I had ever loved or slept with, every girl I'd ever known and thought, With which of these will I get me a son?

Her name was Nava. She was a widow, married six months to a dashing fighter pilot who had been killed over the canal the first day of the war. I paid her a condolence call. There were many such condolence call weddings that took place in Israel that first year after the war.

I married her because I wanted children and I thought she would be the best person to do that with.

She married me because I wasn't a hero.

Her first husband, the one she really loved, madly loved, was the dashing and daring young man in the flying machine, with his turned-up collar on his flight jacket and gorgeous face and body. He was the young prince of Israel.

I was the frog.

Women had found that while we might not be

as tall nor as handsome, we tended not to get killed.

I was, after my brief brush with the foul-breathed grim-visaged angel, a jobnik once again. A traffic cop in the military police. A meter maid more or less. It was a nine-to-five gig.

I would be based in Tel Aviv, not Sinai, and the enemy I faced was usually no more fearsome than the kid who stole a Jeep for the weekend to visit his girlfriend.

I was boring. Therefore I would survive.

I was a Volvo, not a Ferrari.

We were married for three years.

She couldn't have children.

Our marriage ended when I found she was having an affair with an El Al pilot. He had been in her first husband's squadron during the war. He had come to pay a condolence call.

What's the old saying? You want to make God laugh?

Tell him your plans.

But the point was, I knew exactly what Schvester Rochelle was talking about. At one age, when faced with the moment of death you want nothing more than to be back inside your mother's womb.

That's what Chad was feeling when Jack put his gun on him and said, "I think we need to talk."

At another age, when faced with death and having survived it, you want nothing more than to *have* children.

Thus it is perhaps understandable that Jack, when faced with the knowledge true and certain that his wife and her young lover were indeed plotting his own death, should have felt perhaps a similar urge, the need to have a son, or at least to confess that indeed he already had one.

"Chad," he said, the gun still trained upon the boy, "I am your father."

Seven

"Whoa, shit," said Chad.

"You've said a mouthful, sonny," Jack said, smiling not at all unkindly at the young man who shivered noticeably in the wind that had begun to come in off the ocean, blowing the clouds across what was left of the sun. The sky was purple now, deep wine grape purple and black like a bruise across the sky, as if God were a mean drunk who had just smacked Creation around a little.

"No way," Chad said, shaking his head back and forth in counterpoint to the way his body shook now from the cold.

"Way indeed," said Jack. Then he motioned with the gun for Chad to dry off. "Better towel yourself, sonny. You'll catch your death."

"Hey, man, I, like, don't even know you so . . ."

"Sonny, dry off," Jack said. "Remember, Father knows best."

"Stop sayin' that," Chad said, but he grabbed the towel nonetheless and rubbed at the wet gooseflesh.

"Stop saying what?"

"Stop saying that sonny shit. I mean I don't know who you think I am, mister, but—"

"Sonny, please, surely there's no need to call me mister," Jack said interrupting him.

But it was as if Chad didn't hear or rather could not both speak and process that which he had heard at the same time. So he decided to continue speaking and ignore anything else until his own hard-won thought had been completed and vocalized.

"I mean I don't know who you think I am, mister, but . . ."

"But what?" Jack asked gently, as if prodding a slow-witted child.

"But, well, I'm not," Chad said clutching the towel around his shoulders. "I'm not whoever you think I am."

"I think," Jack said very evenly, "that you're the young man who is defiling my wife and plotting with her to murder me for my insurance."

"Whoa, shit," said Chad.

"Please don't say that again, sonny, it's growing tiresome. Get in the car . . . slowly."

Jack motioned with the gun for Chad to get

into the car. Jack held the door open in one hand and kept his gun on the younger man with the other.

Chad was fighting hard now to filter the myriad thoughts that ran through his brain at once and distill them into a single course of action. The thoughts that skipped across the synapses, that raced with electric charges and chemical reactions from one cell to the other went something like this:

OhshitohshitohshitohshitRUNNNNNN!!!!!!!

He thought about slamming the door on his tormentor's hand as he had seen movie stars do in any number of the action films he so loved to watch when he was stoned. He thought of grabbing, punching, throwing, biting, crying, begging, killing, running, crawling. He saw himself doing all of these things in his own mind's eye and in some scenarios he was wildly successful and in others he was lying beside the car writhing in pain, holding the ends of intestines which had just been shot through by the thirty-eight. His knees were knocking, actually knocking, physically knocking so loud he thought the whole world could hear them. He was freezing and yet he was sweating. He could feel the drop of icy sweat slide from armpit to rib cage and he thought again of curling up someplace safe and dark and warm away from Jack and the gun that would kill him as soon as he got into the car. The thoughts all ran together until he could not sort one from the other and quite simply could not move. The circuits are jammed, he thought, and that thought only added to the confusion, until joining with all the other messages being screamed aloud in his brain he heard now a new voice, at once feminine and mechanical that said, I'm sorry, all lines are busy now, please hang up and try your call again later.

"Sonny," he heard Jack say as if from a long way off.

"What?" Chad finally managed to say.

"Don't think about running and don't think about fighting. Just get in the car and you'll be safe."

Chad still could not move, whether paralyzed from fear or indecision Jack could not tell.

"Sonny," he said again calmly, as if trying to soothe the boy with dispassionate authority, "look at me."

Chad did not respond.

"Look at me, son," Jack said again in a kind, fatherly voice. "Look at my hand. It's not shaking. Listen to your voice quivering. Look at your knees the way they knock together, look at how you shiver. Who are you going to trust? What voice are you going to listen to? Yours, which is so frightened, or mine, which is so sure? I know what I'm doing, son. Trust me and get into the car. If I wanted to kill you, don't you think you'd be dead already? Get into the car. I know what I'm doing. You're not thinking clearly now. I am. Trust me."

Chad slid into the car. He slid across the front

seat over to the driver's side, and his wet bathing suit scrunched up into his crotch.

"You got a wedgie?" Jack asked as he slid in beside him. "It's okay, pull your pants down."

"Whoa, shit," Chad said.

"I don't mean pull them down like that. I mean so you're comfortable. I want you to be comfortable," Jack said, pointing the thirty-eight still at the right side of Chad's head.

Chad pulled down at his bathing suit.

"That's better, eh?" Jack asked, "Comfy? I hate those wedgie things."

"Yeah," said Chad.

"There, see?" Jack asked. "We're having a conversation now. Isn't that nice? Not so bad. Not so frightening. Isn't that so?"

The clouds had rolled in thick across the sliver of sun and there was no sunset, as if a purple curtain had been suddenly drawn and it was dark, there in the car, no light between them, no sun, no stars, no moon yet, nothing but the yellow glow of headlights in the distance that swept across the black top in a whoosh and was gone.

"Cigarette?" Jack asked, and his voice reminded Chad of one of those Nazis in the Humphrey Bogart flicks you saw at two in the morning when you were stoned as Chad almost always was by that time of night. Cigarette? That's what they always asked and they always had those really cool cigarette cases or they asked for your papers. Papers?

they would ask, and if he was in bed with a girl and they were stoned he'd ask, Papers? And he'd mean the papers they rolled their dope in, and the girl would laugh and so would he.

"Chad, concentrate!" Jack said, poking Chad in the ribs with the muzzle of the gun. It snapped Chad back to the front seat of his car from wherever he was in his mind that still was refusing to focus.

"Take a cigarette. Calm down," Jack said. "And listen."

Then Chad was back. He took the cigarette and in the red glow that danced in the darkness between them, the red glow of the car's lighter that Jack offered him across the darkness, he came back to where he was . . . in deep shit.

"Okay, Mr. Wolfe," Chad said, "Okay."

"*Mister* Wolfe? All things considered I don't think there's a need for such formality, do you? We have so much in common after all. My wife, for instance. I mean you don't call my wife Mrs. Wolfe, do you? You're not like Benchamen Bradduck in the Graduate, I hope. You don't call her Mrs. Robinson, do you?"

"Uh, no," Chad said.

"No, of course not. You call her Nora, or baby, or *oooo baby*, huh? Isn't that right, son?"

"Listen," Chad said, believing he understood now what this was all about. "I'll never see her again, okay? I mean, like, you know, she came on to me and, like, but it's over, okay? I'll tell her. I won't see her again. Ever. I'll move. I was gonna move anyway, but, so it's cool, okay?"

"But why?" Jack asked as if he couldn't believe his ears. "Why should you do such a thing? She's a really wonderful piece of ass, isn't she? And I don't care. Honestly. I'm the one who suggested it. I couldn't be more pleased."

"What father doesn't dream of his son following in his footsteps, though it's not exactly my feet that you're following in this case, is it? But still, you know what I mean, don't you son?"

He's out of his fucking mind, Chad thought to himself, wacked out of his mind. This old guy must have been into some really *heavy* shit. Like opium or somethin'.

"I'm not crazy, Chad," Jack said softly.

Chad just about shit. It occurred to him then that:

A) Either he had somehow spoken aloud that which he imagined he had only thought, or
B) Jack could read his mind.

Either way, Chad nearly lost it.

"Calm down, son," Jack said in that fatherly tone of voice. "Let me explain to you some things about life. About the way life really is and not how it looks on the television or in the movies or stories, you know?"

It was as if Chad was a virgin. Timid, frightened, terrified in fact and yet at the same time somehow assured by an older man who talked in such a soothing voice that he fascinated Chad. Older, wiser, surer, Jack was seducing him as surely as he had the young, dark-skinned girls in Mozambique, as surely as he had seduced Nora once as well.

"First, you should know," Jack said, sucking on his own cigarette, glowing brighter than fading there beside Chad in the darkness, "I have to die. One way or the other at least on paper, you see? I've gotten myself into some financial difficulties and, well, the only way for me to avoid prison and poverty, which in and of itself is a kind of prison too, is it not, is to die, to be declared legally dead. So as they say in Appalachia, either you're with me or agin me. If you leave now, I'll make sure it looks to that Chewish cop who arrested you that you were behind my murder. I'll make it look like your leaving was in fact part of the murder plan."

It's just like Nora said, Chad thought, either way I'm screwed.

"So," Jack said, "either way you're screwed."

Chad about lost control of his bowels once again.

"But listen," he said. "It doesn't have to be that way. I promise you. I've planned for this for a long time, since before you, since before Nora, since before you were born in fact, son."

He took another drag on the cigarette.

"When I was a much younger man, over thirty

years ago now, I realized that there might come a time when because of the way I lived my life I might have to disappear. I haven't been entirely honest in the way I've made my living I'm afraid, you know. So I thought even then, well, there may come a time when the police are closing in and then I'm going to have to vanish, cease to exist, at least on paper. But just because I'm going to die doesn't mean I can't make some money out of it. Or perhaps, especially since I'm going to die, there must be a way to make some money out of it. And so I had myself insured. Enough money to make sure that after my death I could live very comfortably. But then, who to leave it to? To whom could I leave this vast sum of money? For it had to be someone whom I could trust with, well, with my life and more important, my money."

Jack waited, perhaps hopefully for Chad to contribute something, but when Chad finally spoke it was only to say, "You got another cigarette?"

"Sure," said Jack happily. "You like them, son? They're Rothmans."

"Yeah," said Chad as he accepted the cigarette. He would rather have had a Marlboro but Chad thought, as his mother once told him, it wouldn't cost him anything to be nice, especially to someone who was holding a gun on him. Chad lit the cigarette off the proffered lighter.

"Well," Jack said, "so who could I trust? A woman? A lover, well I think you and I have both seen how inconsistent they can be, eh, my boy?"

"No shit," Chad said almost involuntarily, surprised at the sound of his own voice.

"No shit indeed, my boy," Jack said with glee as if Chad had pronounced some heretofore undiscovered universal truth. "No shit indeed. I can see why Nora chose you. Not chust the body, the wit! So of course it can't be a lover. But then what? A parent? I must confess I engineered my own father's murder so he certainly wasn't going to be of much help. And my mother? Well, she helped me get rid of my father, so who was going to trust her? I had one person who worked for me going all the way back to my boyhood in Shanghai, but he was an Oriental. So there we are. Who to trust? And then I realized it. There could be no one else than a devoted child, someone who gave to me the possibility of a trusted and more important dutiful repository for my nest egg. Chad, my boy, I created my own child! It was God-like I promise you. It was Old Testament God-like.

"I but spoke the word and it was done. You understand? No, of course you don't. Look. Usually you create a child, what do you need? Hmmm? Chad, I'm asking, what do you need?"

"Uhh," said Chad. "A woman."

"Yes! Exactly! You need a woman. You need a man. You need a sperm and you need an ovum. You need fertilization to take place and incubation, nine months of whining and all their bullshit, and then the blood and the mess and what do you get out of it? Some squalling, wrinkled thing that takes in from one end and puts out from the other. A refuse machine, nothing more, nothing more. And then you have to raise them and God only knows what until they're good for anything and then how do you ever know? Look at my father and me. You think he didn't die disappointed?"

Jack was silent again. Chad said nothing.

"Chad!" Jack snapped. "I'm asking: You think he didn't die disappointed?"

"He must have been pissed," Chad said reasonably.

"Yes! Pissed! Of course! Exactly! You see it all so clearly. But then, what I did, as I say, as I said before was, was positively God-like. No penis. No pussy. No sperm. Just . . . the word. Let there be a child! And there was one. And behold it was good. I registered a birth. That's all. So simple. Nothing more. At the time there were countries, I dare say there still may be such places, where a woman gives birth, a local peasant girl, and the birth is registered at the town hall or perhaps just a church or some minor government registry. No fingerprint, no footprint, just a fee paid to a commissar, like a dog license and a name set down in a registry. A young girl gives birth to a bastard . . . she's a prostitute maybe, some kind of degenerate, that's for certain, and the bastard dies and so you say to her the baby's birth is a fact, it's been registered, yes? But why register the death as well? Who's to profit from that? Here my child, take this money. Use it to buy your narcotics. I shall step forward and say I cannot keep silent anymore.

"I am the baby's father and I want to legally give it my name. Another fee. Another name in the town registry filled out by another clerk who pockets a little on the side too, eh? And the girl? She vanishes, well, buys some bad dope perhaps and dies. Maybe with a little help. But the child? The child lives! There is a birth certificate after all and with that you can get a passport and once there is a passport and a birth certificate, once there is citizenship and the child is entered in the rolls of loyal countrymen of not one but three European nations, who can doubt that the child lives? The education? I say I kept my offspring at home and hired tutors. I was the one who took all the matriculation exams. I'm afraid Jean—that's the name I chose—was not much of a scholar. Well, the acorn doesn't fall far from the tree, eh? When Jean reached the age of eighteen, an apartment was rented. Cars were bought. Credit cards were applied for and issued, purchases are regularly made and bills are promptly paid. Jean was raised in Switzerland. Marvelous country. Anything is possible there if the records are kept well enough. The Swiss, God bless them. Who else could have invented the cuckoo clock, eh? A fake bird with his counterfeit chirp every hour, precisely on the hour? Jean exists, legally exists and can inherit my money, and what do you think? Jean and Nora are now the sole beneficiaries on my insurance policy. And if Nora is guilty of my murder, then Jean will receive the death benefit once I have been killed. Chad, I say, *you* are Jean. I say Jean is an empty mold into which I can pour whatever I choose, and I choose you, my good son. I will give you what you need, the account numbers, the identity papers, credit cards, medical histories, I will teach you what you need to know in order to convince the bank in Liechtenstein which will receive the death benefit in trust for Jean, that you and Jean are one in the same. Think to yourself a moment, son, can you trust Nora? She's a wonderful piece of tail that's true, a great sexual athlete, but would you trust her with your life? I certainly wouldn't. And I've known her a good deal longer than you have. My boy, she is screwing us both, literally and figuratively. I tell her, find Chad and we'll fake my death and frame him and split the insurance. She tells you that you and she will *really* kill me and then she'll split the insurance with *you*. Well you know what? She's going to have the best of all possible worlds! I'll be dead. You'll be framed for it and she'll keep all the money herself! Think of her. You know I'm telling you the truth. Fuck her by all means. But you can't trust her and you know it. So I say, you and I, my son, we will be each other's salvation. We will fake my death and split the insurance, and the two of us will frame Nora!"

Eight

"Idiot!"

"Idiot!" That's what she would say, Chad
thought as he walked from where Jack had let him
off on Front Street down past Kimo's and the T-
shirt shops and the galleries that sold their little
prints of whales and dolphins swimming beneath
and above the surface of the water with Lahaina
bathed in happy light and all the creatures of the
sea and earth living in symbiotic harmony.

Well, Chad didn't use the word symbiotic in his
thoughts, they were more along the lines of all the
fish and shit . . . but the point was you never saw
a shark. There were no man-eaters in those pictures. You didn't see the seven caves where they
slept or the water churning where they ripped the

flesh. Chad knew the sea. He was a diver and a surfer and a deckhand, and a shark had almost taken his fingers off when he gaffed it for a tourist while he worked for Larsen, the old Norwegian skipper of the forty-footer he crewed on when the fishing was good and they needed extra help. He knew the sea wasn't anything like the pictures they printed on posters and calendars and coffee mugs and T-shirts with save the whales slogans and addresses for donations to Greenpeace on them.

He knew the sea was all about eating and being eaten, killing before you were killed, little fish swallowed by big ones, torn apart by bigger ones still, who would turn and feed on themselves if there was nothing else to kill and the frenzy were on them. He knew that was the absolute truth about the sea. It was a place of constant killing and without it, there was no life. Get in the sea and if you stay in or on it long enough, eventually the sea will kill you. You could take that one to the bank. You could place the long-haul bet on that and never lose. It was the one sure thing in town.

Once they had gone out on the *Mariner,* which was the name of Larsen's boat. They had a man and his kid from the mainland who bought the boat for the day to go out fishing. It was clear and the water was flat when they left in the morning with the sun hanging up there like a french fry light on the water, Chad thought. You have your metaphors, Chad had his.

Then the wind kicked up. You could see it first on the foam atop the crests of water that crossed diagonally across the bow, grew in size and definition, intensity and speed, with flecks of foam that spit out atop the waves like saliva in the air as the water's color changed from clear and blue as sudden as a thunderstorm to black. It would hit them soon, the old Norwegian said.

"Fishing's over, boys," he said and sounded, Chad thought, just like Lawrence Welk when he was a kid and his grandfather used to watch that crap.

Larsen turned the boat back toward Lahaina. He knew the man from the mainland would be pissed about the day's charter, and perhaps hoping to entertain him so that he would still pay full fare, he told a story. Or perhaps it was because Larsen himself grew pensive when the sea was like this; black and hard with Hawaii's light covered over as if it never existed while it waited for the storm.

"The sea can kill you," he said. "That's why we're heading back. You can't just think because you're on vacation, you know? The sea's a great big son of a bitch. When I was a young man," he said, and whether for theatrics or because he really was lost in thought, he stared out toward the horizon that melted now, grey-black into the sea. "When I was a young man I used to work the fishing boats in the North Sea, God Jesus that was cold, and there was one Christmas where we picked up a Mayday. It was a freighter maybe fifty miles to the north of us and they were sending out a Mayday. It was Christmas and they were sinking and it was so cold the doors and windows to the pilot house were frozen shut. But it didn't matter anyway, because they were sinking fast and with it so cold as that, they wouldn't have survived. I was on the watch and I heard as one by one, they came to the radio and dictated their wills and then it was quiet, except for the static. We never found a trace of them. It was Christmas."

The old Norwegian said nothing more until they sighted land, and in the cockpit of the forty-footer it wasn't a vacation fishing trip anymore. It was for them a freezing Christmas in the cold North Sea, so cold the doors and windows were freezing shut and they waited, it seemed for the silence to be broken as if hoping even now fifty years later and two oceans away the silence would end with someone saying they were safe, had not sunk, had not been swallowed whole by the sea and drowned on Christmas.

"Land," said the old Norwegian skipper who had left the frozen waters of his native island for this sunny one as if that would keep him safe.

They had been lucky, or perhaps Larsen was that skillful. They had beaten the storm back to land.

It broke, awful and violent as a child-abusing drunk in a rage crashing itself against the island again and again, ripping trees like children's toys up out of the earth and throwing them in a tantrum across the highway. But even so, Chad thought, when you get to land you're safe.

That's the way he thought of it. Land was safe. Only the sea could kill you, or maybe some bad dope, but if you knew who you bought from and weren't an asshole and never did really hard shit or used dirty needles or fucked with a Samoan, if you got to land you were safe.

It was just the sea that could kill you and land was where the parties were. But now he had met Jack Wolfe and Nora and he knew that wasn't true.

She'd be pissed. She'd called him an idiot and maybe slap him and maybe this time he'd hit her, deck her, you know? Cause what's that, huh? Callin' him stupid, what's that? But anyway, if he hit her or he didn't, sooner or later she'd come over and grab his dick. That's how it always ended with her. She made it up to him if she was mean.

Besides, maybe this was cool. Maybe—hey, no *maybe* about it—now she *had* to see this whole thing was bogus, man. I mean, he was on to them. He was waiting for them, both of them and, like, now he wanted him to help double-cross her? Like he would do that shit? Like he would fall for that shit? But the point was, everybody knew every-thing! So they'd call it off.

She'd be pissed. She might even hit him and then he'd whack her and she'd grab his dick and it would be cool, cause this was fuckin' crazy, man! This was nuts! I mean like maybe they really were smart and shit, but this was flat out, full tilt goofy.

So going up to his apartment, climbing the stairs up from the street to his funky little apartment, he felt just like he always did when he got to dry land.

"Was that my husband, Chad?" he heard her voice say in the darkness.

Chad just about shit.

"Jesus fuckin' Christ, Nora!" He reached for the light and tripped over his sneakers and an empty Coors can that was lying on the floor.

"Where are you? How the fuck can you see in the dark? What are you a fuckin' salamander or somethin'? Shit," he said. "Shit . . . ouch . . . shit."

He stumbled about until he found the switch and turned it on. She was sitting there in his kitchen chair, which she'd moved over to the window. The ashtray was full next to her. She had no tan. It was weird. It was like all of a sudden she didn't have any tan at all, pale as a lizard's belly.

"Okay, look," he said. "I know you're gonna be pissed."

"I'm not angry, Chad," she said in that low voice of hers that sounded like tiger purrs. "I just want to know, was that my husband? That's a simple enough question."

"Okay," he said, ready for her to call him an idiot and maybe get up and hit him, in which case he'd definitely decided to deck her. He didn't really like her or her husband, he decided. In fact he now realized if she didn't have that body and wasn't such a phenomenal lay, he wouldn't even talk to her. She wasn't very nice.

"Okay," he said. "Yeah, that was your husband. He snuck up on me over at Two Heads Point and then talked a bunch of crazy shit to me and dropped me off on Front Street. I gotta go back for my car tomorrow."

He waited for her to call him an idiot. He waited for her to get up off the chair, cross the room, slap him hard across the mouth, and call him an idiot. He not only waited for it, but had he reflected upon it, he would have found that he anticipated it now, not without some sense of pleasure, because he fully expected that what would follow, as the night does the day, would be the grabbing of his dick part.

"And?" she said.

"Huh?" said Chad.

"And," said Nora, "then what?"

She sat where she was in the chair by the window, calm, cold in fact, not even a little pissed off. She reached for a cigarette and lit it and looked at him curiously.

"Uh," Chad said, "what do you mean *and*? I mean like he's on to us, okay? It's fucked. It's over."

"Nothing's over," she said, looking at her nails and then up at him so cold he felt his scrotum tighten. "What did he say, Chad? Please try to remember exactly. Please try to be specific. Your life and a great deal of money could depend on this."

Chad looked at her and though he could not have explained why he felt the way he felt, he was, in fact, at least as frightened of her as he had been of Jack. And she didn't even have a gun.

"He talked a bunch of crazy shit, okay?" he said quietly.

"What kind of crazy shit, Chad?" she purred.

"What's it matter, Nora?"

"It matters to me, Chad. I'm not kidding about your life depending on this, you know? Jack's a very dangerous man. You need me, Chad. You need me to tell you what he's up to."

"Oh no, man," Chad said and laughed because for once he knew more than her and that equated in Chad's mind with being smarter than her.

"Oh no, man," he said. "You need me."

"Chad," she said and crossed her legs, and even in the dim light he could see that underneath the slit white skirt she was wearing no panties.

He gulped.

She barely smiled.

"What did he say, Chad? Start at the beginning and be as specific as you can and when this is over I'll make you feel better than you've ever felt in your life. I'll do things with my tongue and with ice you never thought were possible. I'll do things for you that you couldn't buy in Vegas for under twenty-five thousand dollars."

Chad gulped. He couldn't even imagine what a woman could do that would cost twenty-five thousand dollars in Vegas. But he was sure Nora knew what those things were and how to do them. This was tangible. Twenty-five thousand dollars' worth of sex for a clear memory.

"Uhh, okay," said Chad, trying to focus as he never had in school. "First he asked me if I had a wedgie . . ."

Thus Chad began an extraordinarily comprehensive recitation of his conversation with Jack Wolfe and it struck him in the middle of his oral history that if any of his teachers in high school had been half the piece of ass that Nora Wolfe was, he could really have amounted to something.

"A kid!" she said when he'd finished. "He left the money to a fucking kid?"

"John," Chad said. "He named the kid John."

"It's bullshit," she said. She sat back and it was as if Chad was no longer in the room, as if the room was no longer in the world. She was gambling now with Jack Wolfe. He was bluffing and this was bullshit.

"Hey," Chad said. "The whole thing's bullshit, okay? So it's over. Let's just . . ."

Nora looked up at him. "Let's just what, Chad?" she asked and there was a real cruelness to the sneer she wore now. "Let's just do what? Continue our . . . what is this . . . our romance? You know what Jack will be doing? He won't be playing with himself every afternoon. He'll be planning. You think this is over for Jack? He doesn't have any choice but to pull this off. Otherwise, he's worse than dead. He's broke. So he'll keep planning and you and I both know what the plan is, don't we? Frame you. That's the name of the plan, Chad. It's called frame you. You leave today and he'll make sure it looks like you hired whoever it was who killed him. There's probably a bank account that's already been opened somewhere in your name. Transfers have probably already been made to would-be assassins. Anything of yours missing, Chad? Ask yourself that the next time you do your laundry."

She looked around the room in disgust.

"Oh, I forgot," she said. "Well, *should* you ever do laundry, you might stop and think . . . is something of mine gone?"

She got up and crossed over to him, taunting him with the way she moved her hips and with the way her legs shone beneath the slit and the way she smelled, which caught him by the nostrils, grabbed him by the throat, and almost seemed to pull him up towards her by his crotch.

"Didn't you tell me you'd lost your pocket knife, Chad? Wasn't that over at my place? You were so upset because you lost that stupid Boy Scout knife."

It was true. Chad had misplaced the knife, one

of the few possessions that held any emotional value for him. It had been over at her place in the white-on-white plantation house she shared with Mr. Wolfe, which was how he thought of him, Mr. Wolfe, like a large, mean, and feared neighbor whose window pane he had just broken.

"Maybe Jack has it, Chad. You think he won't use it, with your fingerprints all over it? You think it won't turn up at the scene of the murder? I promise you it will. So I have a choice, don't I? I can help Jack frame you or I can help you kill Jack. But you . . . you don't have a choice, Chad. You just have one decision. Do you want to spend Jack's money with me on the beach in the Grand Caymans or do you want to check into Hawaii State Penitentiary as playmate of the month? I know a little about being the object of men's desires, Chad. If that's what you decide, I can probably give you some pointers. But you can't choose not to be in this. That's over. That was over the minute I chose you."

Chad wanted to weep. He wanted to cry. Instead, all he did was whine and say, "Why? Jesus, Nora, why? Why do you people do this?"

Nora smiled.

"Like the scorpion said, 'It's our nature'."

The next week Jack left for the mainland and Nora called the security company. It wasn't that the combination on the safe had been changed, the entire safe itself had been removed and replaced with another. She had no idea when it had happened. She explained to the security company that she felt like a fool. That new safe we put in, she said, Jack's away and he left the combination but she can't find it and his watch is in the safe and she wants to have it engraved for their anniversary. It's to be a surprise.

The dumb Portagee-named rep on the phone said he was sorry. He couldn't give out the new combination to anyone but Jack. Then Nora explained that she had the combination but that it wouldn't work. Could they not just send out a technician?

He was a Glen. An earnest young Japanese with pocket protectors who had never gotten this close to a woman like Nora who didn't have a staple through her navel. It was real simple, she said. Her husband would kill her if she didn't get the documents that were in the safe to the bank in time. He would kill her if she had been stupid enough to lose the combination. Thus, she would trade her virtue for young Glen's ability to open the lock. In essence, he would be unlocking two treasures with each twist of the dial. One that would be hers. One that would be his.

Glen came and went. Nora took the policy from the manila envelope in the safe. It was in German but she could read the name Jean Wolfe next to that of her own. There was a little note, a

Post-it tab on the policy. "Dearest Nora," it read. "This is just a copy, so don't think that by destroying this document your problems will have been solved. Now then, who do you think our Chad is going to betray? You or me?"

Nine

"Don't you think, Lovey," Jack said, snorting the line of cocaine that he laid out on the mirrored top of the bar. "Don't you think that our Chad is like the child we never had the chance to abuse?"

He pinched one nostril off and snorted loudly, then bent down and began to suck up the second line through the Happy Meal straw and into his nose.

Nora said nothing. She sat, drinking her vodka, washing down the Xanax with her Absolut at the white table across from the bar that fed out onto the lanai looking out to the ocean and the thick bank of dead, metal gray clouds streaked suddenly yellow with lightning that rolled in, unstoppable now against the island that lay there, waiting to be hit, waiting pliantly as if sprawled upon a bed to be abused.

Her drinking was constant now. It never left her. It offered no solace, it only vaguely dulled the knife of pain that seemed to be slicing permanently now into her skull. She alternated it with Seconal and sometimes Quaaludes.

"You're not a very up person anymore," Chad had said. She had laughed and said, "No shit."

Jack mowed down the line of cocaine, snorting loudly through the children's straw with its clown face twisting its way up into Jack's nostril.

"You're a fucking Hoover," Nora said, throwing back the drink, swallowing down the tranquilizer.

"What's that, Lovey?" Jack asked and pinched off his other nostril now and snorted once, twice, three times, then wet his finger and ran it down the residue on the mirrored top of the bar and licked it noisily.

"A fucking Hoover," Nora said loudly.

Jack ignored her. He looked instead at the mirrored bar top.

"This was such a good idea, you know?" Jack said, running his hand across the mirrored surface of the bar. He wore a wistful look as he said, "I mean when we first put it in I'll admit to you I thought of it only in sexual terms. I pictured, you know, warm nights by the fire and you sitting naked on top of it, maybe not naked, maybe just no panties, like that blonde in the movies. I thought maybe we could have company over and you could sit on the bar top singing torch songs and it could be our private little secret and I could point it out to just a select few of our friends."

Jack let out a long, forlorn sigh. "All those romantic plans," he said and then ran his tongue along the residue of cocaine still left on the mirrored top. "The idealism of youth, all of it gone by, but still it's awfully good for cocaine. Would you like some, Lovey?" he said.

Nora tilted her head towards him. She said nothing, only watched the fresh slash of lightning smack down against the horizon and then rumble up towards them, rattling the glass.

"But you haven't answered me. Don't you honestly think that Chad is like the—"

"No," Nora said drily, "I don't."

"—child we never had?" Jack said, completing the thought in spite of her. "You don't? Really? Because you know, if we had had a child like Chad, he would be bad," said Jack, smiling his wolfy grin. "Wouldn't he?"

"Sam I am," Nora said softly to no one.

"What's that, Lovey?" Jack asked amiably.

"Sam I fucking am," Nora said. "Sam I am. It's American, okay? It's a lovely, American, innocent fucking children's book, okay? So you wouldn't know what I'm talking about."

"Xenophobia, liebschen, tut-tut," Jack said.

The lightning hit again, closer this time, jagging down to the water, lighting up the skies turned black with cloud and roaring at them, carried on the wind that swept in now the first squalls that whipped the palms and picked the patio table up suddenly and threw it into the wall.

"Storm's a-coming," Jack said cheerfully in his fake black/German accent.

They never mentioned the safe or the insurance policy or the note Jack had left for her on it. It was like their own quiet dirty secret, never mentioned, mutually acknowledged, always present, there like a silent tumor left to grow until it squeezed out anything left alive between them, until it consumed their lives, became their lives, was the essence, the purpose, the meaning of their lives now. Jack was right. Chad was their child and they battled for his affections.

"It's Jean, okay?" Nora said to Chad in disgust. "Not John. Got it?"

"What's the difference?" Chad said. He was sulking. They were going to kill him or cause his death or incarceration for life and he knew it and there was nothing he could do about it and he was in a pissy mood because of it.

"It makes a difference because you're going to do exactly what Jack said."

Chad looked up suddenly. Did she mean she wanted him to help Jack frame her, too? He would have believed anything by now. He thought of it in comic book terms. It helped make things clearer to him. He was in bizarro-land now. You know the place where there's a bizarro Superman and a bizarro Clark Kent and a bizarro Lois Lane and a bizarro Jimmy Olsen? Well he was the bizarro Jimmy Olsen and he was fucking Lois.

And then he would think, You know that song about don't step on Superman's cape? So, like, what if he was really a bizarro Jimmy Olsen and Nora was really Lois. What do you think that made Jack Wolfe? Fucking Superman, okay? So what do you think that meant for Jimmy Olsen? It meant he'd better find some fucking Kryptonite fast.

That was as far as he had been able to take it. But it did seem to help him understand things better at a time when nothing made sense at all anymore, at a time when he was completely lost, and the natural order of things, the rules of his own individual party-time universe had changed completely.

"You're going to do exactly what Jack tells you," Nora said, trying to get him to focus.

"But I don't get it," Chad said. His head hurt constantly now, and the only defense he had against the pain was to stay stoned. He had a permanent joint to his lips. He smoked all the time, all the shit he could get his hands on, all the time. and it was never enough to make Jack and Nora go away, disappear on a big green cloud, which is all he wanted them to do. He wanted to take a giant hit on a huge cigar-sized log of a joint, to suck the biggest bong hit doperkind had ever known, to inhale hemp, hash, ganja, weed, grass, shit, drek, maryjane, mj, all the fucking cannabis on the continent, take it all into his lungs, hold it there until his brain exploded, and blow it out, see them there, Ozzie and Harriet on acid and make them fucking float away and leave him alone. It's all he wanted.

"Chad," Nora said, and she snapped her fingers and he was back.

"So, like, I don't get it, you know? What do you mean?" Chad asked.

"I mean you're going to let him show you how to be Jean. You're going to let Jack teach you how to be his son. The son exists, just like he told you. He's a mold, just like he told you. And you're going to let Jack pour you into that mold so the two of us can collect the money. Chad," she said, lowering her face down to him so he could see it, so he could focus on her red-streaked eyes. "Chad, it's the only thing that will save you. It's the only thing that will keep you alive and out of prison."

In retrospect then, that may have been the biggest mistake of all. It was like sending your kid for day care to a registered child molester. It was like entrusting your teenager to a summer camp run by the Manson family. She was sending Chad to learn how to become Jack's son. A chip off the old block.

It seemed necessary of course, for he would have to present himself to some bureaucrat somewhere, produce documents, a passport, perhaps a birth certificate. He would have to show proof not only that the child existed and had a right to inherit his father's insurance benefit, but that he was that child, had always been that child, could inhabit the paper body Jack had designed, give it life and say just as surely as Adam said before he was expelled from Eden, "Here I am."

And what of Jack? He doled it out. Piece by piece, slowly at first. One could almost say innocently. He explained that Jean, having been raised on paper in Switzerland, moved permanently to Nigeria.

"And why of course you ask, did he move to Nigeria?" Jack said to Chad when Chad did not ask, leaving Jack to ask it for him, rather like the legend of the four sons at the Passover seder. There was the good son, the wicked son, the stupid son and the son with no capacity to ask. Chad was somewhere in between stupid and no capacity. So Jack, like the good father in the legend, asked the question for him.

"Why Nigeria? Because," Jack said, smiling at the memory, "the bureaucrats there are as corruptible as the fourteen-year-old girls in Mozambique. It's extraordinary," he said. "Truly extraordinary. For really bargain basement prices you can get any documentation at all. I'm talking passports, driver's license, business licenses, sworn statements from the Minister of Justice himself if you like, attesting to anything. So my Jean moved to Nigeria and owns an import-export business there. You'll get me nice little photos and I will give you a passport in the name of Jean Wolfe, who has dual citizenship—Swiss and Nigerian. I have letters or rather, Jean has them, which is to say you will have them, sent by me from all the places I have lived for three decades, sent for the past years from Hawaii to Nigeria to my beloved Jean, full of filial advice, idle gossip, bits and tidbits of news that fathers share with their grown and devoted children. What a joy you have been to me, Jean. What a comfort. I share with you my innermost thoughts. You'll find our beloved Nora in those letters. And the truth I feel towards her. In fact, you'll find my growing concern that perhaps she does not have my best interests at heart. Perhaps in fact, she means to kill me. Yes, I confided in you that I fear for my life, that my wife is in fact conspiring even now, even as we speak, to have me killed, that she conspires with her young lover, that the two of them I fear will have me murdered."

Chad's head was spinning more than usual. "Well, wait a second," he said with his stoned voice. "I mean, like, that's me, isn't it? I mean, like, I'm the young lover, aren't I? I mean, like, who the fuck am I anyway? If I'm Jean, you know?"

Jack beamed like the father of a precocious child. "Yes," he said. "Of course you see the quandary. It's a sword, my boy. A sword with two edges."

"A double-edged sword," Chad said.

"Yes, precisely so, my child," said Jack almost

in benediction. "A double-edged sword which can slice you," he said, running his long doper pinky fingernail across Chad's throat. "And dice you . . . or make you rich. You see," he explained, "if you present the letters to, let us say, the banker who has always taken care of your finances and who is known to and trusted by the company which issued the insurance policy on my life, if you present those letters to that bureaucrat, they are proof that you are your father's son, Jean, and deserve to get the money. Therefore, that is the one edge which makes you rich. On the other hand, should someone else present those very same letters to the local police, should, let us say, an old and trusted friend of mine, someone unknown to you, Chad, and more specifically, unknown to my lovely wife, Nora, have a copy of those letters and should that old and trusted friend and retainer present those letters to the local police, let us say for instance, to our local gendarme of the Hebrew persuasion, Detective Kahana, think what would happen. Picture it. I am dead and Kahana receives copies of these letters from my trusted friend. Letters from a father to his child confiding his innermost fears that his young wife and her even younger lover are plotting to murder him for the insurance money. Well, that's the other edge, isn't it? That's the one that will slit your throat."

Ten

Jack's teachings had a subtler purpose than just how to fill out the forms necessary to pass Chad off as Jean. Its purpose was slowly, bit by logical bit, to enlist Chad as a confidante, to win his heart, to turn him from his lover, Nora, to his newfound father, Jack.

"It's positively Shakespearean or Greek or both," Jack would say to Nora. "I send you to a lover and I make him my son. I hope you appreciate it, Lovey, all the delicious Oedipal delights I give you."

And to Chad, he would say just as Nora had said, "I am your salvation." He made a very compelling case of it.

"Think of it," he would tell Chad as the latter

smoked the dope Jack got for him, the really wonderful primo shit that made Chad say, "Whoa,
thanks, man."

"Think of it," Jack would tell him. "Let us say
you do what Lovey wants. Kill poor Jack, kill the
man who holds his hand out to you now like a loving father. Chad, truly I'm stretching my hand out
to you man to man, like a father to a son. So let us
say you and Lovey kill me. And let us say I am
right. What does she do?"

Jack waited for an answer.

Chad smoked.

"Chad," Jack said gently.

"Yeah," Chad said. "I'm listening, man."

"Yes, all right, well, I was hoping you might be
talking too, but be that as it may, let us say you and
Lovey kill me. Let us say I am right. What does
Lovey do? She frames *you*," Jack said, pointing at
Chad so he would know whom he meant by the
word *you*.

"She frames you," he said again, touching
Chad's chest just above his heart. "She goes to her
Chewish cop and she says, 'My God, look what
happened. It got out of hand. The boy was obsessed with me and look what tragedy came out of
it.' So, you go to jail with great big homosexuals.
You know?"

He let that hang there in the air between them
with the smoke that curled and circled slowly from
Chad's joint.

"That's not what I want for you, Chad. But let's

say you don't believe me. And I'm not saying you're wrong, son. I respect your intelligence. *I* don't think you're stupid."

"Nora does," Chad said petulantly, like a teenaged boy complaining about his stepmother.

"Well," said Jack, bonding for the moment with his wife's young lover, "what does she know? She can be vicious. You don't need to tell me. I know."

"No shit," said Chad, sucking in another hit, nodding his head in agreement.

"No," Jack said, nodding in time to Chad's nodding head, "no shit indeed. So I respect your intelligence and if you say to me, 'Oh no, Nora's not going to betray me,' then I believe you."

Chad looked at Jack narrowly. He was trying to figure out if he had in fact said that to Jack. He had heard it and it was actually what he believed. He just didn't know which of them had said it.

"Well," Jack said, as if he could read Chad's mind. "What difference does it make? Let's say you're right. Let's say you kill poor old Jack who treats you like his son because Nora's such a wonderful sexual athlete and she's promised to spend all my money with you in Tahiti."

"The Grand Caymans," Chad said, and then covered his mouth as if he'd said a no-no and divulged Nora's secret.

"The Grand Caymans are nice," said Jack agreeably. "Let's say the Grand Caymans, okay? Chust for the sake of argument, let's say Nora tells you, We'll kill poor old Jack and then spend his money screwing our brains out, smoking dope and drinking in the Grand Caymans. Sounds good, right?"

"No shit," Chad said again.

"Sure, I mean I would go too if I were invited, if I wasn't dead and financing the whole thing. But what happens then, you know? Think past the first joint and the first party on the beach. Think to the next week and the next week and the next week after that. I wouldn't grow tired of you, Chad, I can tell you that right now. Speaking as a man of course, if I were a woman, I wouldn't grow tired of you, but you know Nora. I mean, I don't think, you know, that her nickname is Old Faithful. You know what I mean?"

Chad was looking straight into Jack's eyes now, held there like a snake by a charmer who sways in time to music he cannot hear. "Yeah," Chad said, nodding. "Yeah, I know what you mean. You mean like she'd fuck around on me."

"Well of course, yeah, sure," Jack said in that voice that sounded to Chad so much like Lawrence Welk . . . or Hitler. Or some other German. "It's her nature."

Chad scratched his head. He had heard that phrase before. Nora, yeah. She said that thing about nature. This guy knew his stuff.

"It's only a matter of time, my boy, as exciting as you no doubt are, before her attention will wander. You and I both know that's true. She'll want someone else. And what will happen then? Eh, son?"

Chad leaned back, inhaled the acrid smoke, filled his lungs with it, held his breath, and tried to hold the thought. What would happen then? What would happen then? Then what? Then *what*? He lost it. The thought was gone. Then what what?

"What will happen," Jack gently prodded, "when Nora grows tired of you?"

"Right, right," Chad said happily. He had it back again. "She'll dump me, man." *That* was it. He had it now. "Shit yeah, she'll dump me."

"Yes," said Jack, nodding. "That's certainly a possibility. She may dump you. But ask yourself a question. Who else knows but you that she is guilty of murder?"

"Uhhh," Chad said.

"Let me rephrase it," said Jack. "*No one* but you knows that she is guilty of murder. Isn't that true?"

"Yeah," Chad said, agreeing suddenly. "Yeah," he said with growing vehemence.

"So what do you think our Nora will do under those circumstances? Do you think she'll just dump you? Do you think she'll just give you back your ring or whatever it is that you have between you? Do you think she'll just say, 'Chad, you know I really don't think this relationship is going anywhere'? or 'Chad, I really think I need my space,' and that will be that? Do you think it will just be, you know, breaking up is so hard to do and that's it? You're the person who can put her in jail and she knows it." Jack poked Chad in the chest once again.

"Whoa, shit," Chad said.

"Yes, I should say so," Jack agreed. "Now let me ask you something. Let's say Nora decides as I think you will agree she will, that she has to eliminate you, by which I mean to say, kill you. Let's say that's the situation."

"Okay," said Chad. He was genuinely worried now. He had even put down the joint. "Okay," he said, trying with all his might to focus on the problem at hand.

"Now," said Jack, "I don't want to offend you, but don't you think that Nora is smarter than you?"

Jack paused and seeing the hint of hurt in Chad's eyes he spoke quickly, leaning forward, touching Chad's arm in a comforting gesture.

"Perhaps smarter isn't the right word. You know, English isn't my first language and I have trouble sometimes saying what I really mean. What I really mean is cunning. Grant me, won't you, that Nora has a kind of low cunning, a gutter kind of intellect, a whore's intelligence that gives her a certain advantage over any man, no matter how smart he is? Especially a younger man, like yourself for instance."

"Yeah," said Chad, trying to keep up his end of things. It was hard for him to talk, but he knew that everything Jack was saying was true. Nora was smart. Nora was smarter than him. He was stupid. Nora wasn't.

"So let us say," Jack said, "thus for the sake of argument, that Nora tires of you, that she decides to dump you, but realizing that you are the only one who knows she is guilty of murder and therefore can put her in jail, she decides to eliminate you. She decides to kill you. And we've both just admitted that she is more cunning than you. What kind of chance do you think you'll have against her then? And let me ask one other thing. If the answer is that you won't have that good a chance against her then, wouldn't you have a better chance now?"

Chad looked at him blankly. Jack had gone too fast and he knew it.

"Let us say," Jack said slowly, "that sitting there in the Grand Caymans, after you've screwed each other's brains out and party, party, party, yes, that our beloved Nora grows tired of you, though God only knows how she could, and let us further say she wants to dump you and then she thinks, Oh no, Chad is the one who knows I am guilty of murder. Chad is the one who can have me put into jail for life, I've got to . . ."

"I've got to kill Chad," Chad said.

"Just so," said Jack. "The penny has dropped, eh, my boy? She thinks to herself, I've got to kill Chad. And you grant me her low cunning, her street wisdom so to speak, you grant me that much, yes? So. Now the question is this. Compare the two situations. Situation number one has poor Chad alone, off his home territory in the Grand Caymans, which by the way, Nora knows quite well, I assure you. Ask her if you don't believe me. She lived there once when she was younger, with an embezzler. So it's her territory, with her connections. She's probably slept with the local chief constable. He'll probably do anything for her, the white goddess, you know?"

Chad knew. Chad knew only too well.

"So, my boy," Jack said, "you are in the Grand Caymans where Lovey is making the big nasty with the chief of police and she decides it is time to kill you. To whom do you turn my boy, hmmm?"

Jack waited for an answer.

None was forthcoming.

"Who is your ally against this black widow spider, hmm? Who gives you the good counsel, the sound advice? Who is the one who takes you in hand and guides you and says, Watch out for this, watch out for that. Who does that for you, my son. I ask you, who?"

"Uhh," Chad said. "I don't know."

"Of course you don't," said Jack, commiserating with Chad's sorry predicament. "You don't know a soul on the Grand Caymans, do you?"

"Uhh, nobody except Nora," Chad said.

"And she wants to kill you, so that's no help then is it?" Jack asked not unkindly.

"No," said Chad, his anxiety growing over being

alone in the strange islands where Nora was shtupping the chief constable.

"No," Jack said, "of course not. So there in the Grand Caymans with Lovey wanting to kill you and she with her friends and you with no one, what kind of chance will you have against her, eh? What kind of chance will you have then to stay alive if she wants you dead, which we've both already agreed is exactly how she will want you. What kind of chance, Jean?"

"Close to none," Chad said and felt a genuine wave of sadness wash over his oh-so-stoned body and soul. He was going to die in the Grand Caymans. Lovey would kill him and the chief of police would cover for it because she would promise to do for him things that would normally cost a zillion dollars in Las Vegas.

"Don't look so sad," Jack said in soothing tones of encouragement. "Don't look so sad, mein kindt. Now ask yourself another question, and I promise you the answer will be a more hopeful one."

Chad lifted his eyes to Jack and Jack spoke like Santa promising sugar plums to a street urchin.

"What kind of chance do you stand against Nora if you decided to take action against her now, *before* she has the chance to kill you in the Grand Caymans? What kind of chance do you have against her if you are not alone, but have me on your side? Hmm?"

Chad looked at Jack suspiciously. Jack was probably up to no good, Chad thought.

"But you're probably asking yourself," Jack whispered, "why should I trust this fellow Jack? Why should I trust him and betray my Lovey, Nora? After all, Jack doesn't have a nice wet sex organ which he lets me play with. Jack doesn't make me howl like a hound dog at the moon. So why should I trust him? Because, my boy, you've got to think with your head, with the big head, not the kleiner kopf, the little head, eh? You can trust me because if I grow tired of you, so what? Will I dump you? How shall I dump you, when I am dead? How can you have anything to fear of me? I'm the dead guy! I can't very well rise up from the grave and go to the police and betray you before I collect the money which you're going to inherit, because then who will inherit it for me, eh? So the only danger I pose to you is after you've gotten the money. How then do you protect yourself from me, as if you would need to protect yourself from me, your loving poppa? I tell you how. You meet with the banker in Liechtenstein who has run your finances for you since you reached your maturity. He has never met you, dealt with you only through the mails. You meet him, establish your bona fides and then collect the money, but you tell him you want half the money transferred to an account for your lover, Berendt. You are a homosexual and Berendt is waiting for his money which he must retrieve at the appointed time in Vaduz. I am Berendt. I must be in Vaduz when you are Liechtenstein, otherwise I will not be able to get my half of the money."

"Thus, while I am in Vaduz receiving the transfer you have sent me, I cannot be a threat to you in Liechtenstein. You take your money and you vanish. If you double-cross me and my transfer doesn't come through, I call the police on you. But in so doing, I still will not be able to take the money from you. I will only be able to get even for the double cross. I am willing to trust you, my boy, to trust that for you, as for me, half a loaf will be better than none, and that the two of us can trust each other because it is to neither of our advantages to betray the other. Unlike Nora, I can't fear you will betray me because I'm already dead. And with the mechanism I have suggested, I cannot betray you unless I want to prevent myself from getting my half of the money."

Chad thought he understood. Jack wouldn't fuck him because Jack was already dead. Nora on the other hand would because he knew she had killed Jack.

"So," said Jack, sensing the younger man's comprehension, "with whom do you have a better chance for survival? Who must betray you and who cannot betray you? With which of us is there death and with which of us is there life, with your lover . . . or your poppa?"

Chad looked down and then up into Jack's eyes.

"Poppa," he said softly.

Eleven

Now it was Nora's turn.

The tropical storm had been upgraded to a hurricane and the winds howled incessantly, mournfully. They howled like a mother for a dying child, like a nymphomaniac at a gang bang, like a killer killing, like a victim dying. The winds howled and pulled the palms up at their roots like a mad-woman tearing at her hair. They thrashed the is-land, beat it senseless, brutalized it, but after three days still had not spent themselves against it. They pounded and pounded and it seemed as if their fury grew the more furiously they threw them-selves against her. Nora had known a few men like that. Their beatings fed on beatings and the sight of blood only excited them to beat some more.

This storm was like that. The island like a poor skinny hooker without a pimp to protect her, or a hooker who had crossed her pimp and now was being taught, being broken, being gentled with fists and whips and sap gloves, hoods and horrible objects that pushed and flayed and ripped the flesh as the hurricane now trashed Kaanapali like a wacked-out rock star at the Chelsea.

And now it was her turn with Jack.

He seemed to wait and watch as the hurricane took its toll not only on the coastline and beaches, the hotels and condo resorts and fish restaurants and singles bars, but on Nora as well. There was nothing she could drink that would block out the sound of the winds, no drugs to dull the howling madman cries that echoed out of heaven as if all the angels had gone insane.

"You know, Lovey," he said, "our Chad is making beautiful progress. I can see why you found him so attractive. There's a real eagerness there once he gets the hang of things."

"Oh yeah?" she asked, leering at him with eyes that seemed ready to drip blood they were so streaked with it. "Which one of you was on top?"

"So crude, Lovey," Jack said, filling her glass with more vodka. "So coarse. It used to be quite attractive I must admit. What a glorious piece you were. Care for a twist?"

"Please."

She sat at the bar and Jack was behind it like your favorite bartender, ready with a willing ear, a smile, a wink, a nod of encouragement, the cheapest psychotherapist in the world, a father confessor offering up Absolut instead of absolution.

"Really, Lovey," he said, "what a special combination you were. That face so young, younger than anyone I ever met I think, and that filthy mouth, that wonderful coarseness that ran counterpoint to your lovely, youthful skin. Now the skin and the language have begun to match."

Nora tried not to betray that she was indeed looking at herself in the mirrored bar top and thinking much the same thing. Jack had but given voice to her thoughts. She *had* been beautiful once, and so young.

"You know, it doesn't seem fair?" said Jack. "You and I indulge, even just a little and the skin around the eyes is puffy, it sags here, is sallow there, loose where once it was so tight, like Chad . . . remarkably tight body. Gorgeous. I could like his skin myself, like a juicy Thanksgiving turkey, you know, so firm and moist, and when you slice it the fluid runs along the fresh cut edge. He told me about the Grand Caymans, nice choice. Beautiful young people there."

Nora looked up, watching him now. Her head seemed so heavy, but she was determined not to let Jack see how precariously it seemed to hang from her neck, as if by a thread.

"Interesting thing, this business of murder," he said, lowering his head so his eyes and Nora's were level. "Like anything else I suppose, the more you do it, the easier it is. I'm sure the way you've got it planned, Chad will be the one to actually kill me. I'm assuming you'll be someplace nice and public when it happens, so as to establish an absolute—" He clicked her glass when he said absolute. "So as to establish an absolute air-tight alibi. Yes, I'm sure that's what you have in mind. You want the dirty work done. Let Chad do it of course. I don't blame you. He's like a wonderful sexual bellboy, isn't he? Take my bags up to the room, put the big one over there and hang the hanging bag and hang my husband while you're at it. Poor Chad. Cinderfella. I think he might be starting to resent you, you know, Lovey? It's none of my business, of course. But I think I detect real resentment building there."

"Do you?" It was all she could manage. She was beginning to feel numb and even the winds were seeming now to die down. Only Jack's voice was the same.

"Yes. Of course from his point of view, I suppose, well, as I say, it's not for me to criticize your management style but you know he does sulk a bit, doesn't he? A petulant young man. I mean, here he is taking all the risk killing me and you know, poor chap, he's terrified of me, I think. And then of course he has to pose as Jean. Again he has to do the work, take the risk, and all for what? Because his lover, the older woman if you will, has gotten him into it. I had a much older lover when I was his age. Not as old as you of course, Lovey, about thirty-five. I think I was eighteen, could be twenty, and at first, well, there was nothing that could possibly have been more exciting.

"You know, an older woman who knows these wonderful techniques and positions and wants it so much, not like a young girl, you know, and, as I say nothing on earth was as exciting as that . . . in the beginning. But then of course, well, young boys are so fickle, aren't they? After a while, the very thing that had attracted me began to positively repel me. She suddenly seemed so . . . I don't know . . . so wrinkled. Sagging everywhere really, with the first signs of what do you call it . . . turkey flesh at her neck? The breasts weren't really firm. They were like, well I suppose if I were an optimist I would have said the sack was half-full, but as it was . . . like two half-empty bota bags. And she had a certain smell about her. Like rotting fish. Pungent. Once that pungency was absolutely"—here he clinked her glass again—"an aphrodisiac, but now it smelled like death really. I began to despise her. The touch of her, the way she was so hungry . . . I loathed it now and longed for someone my own age, or younger preferably. Someone nubile, sixteen, a dewy bud instead of a fading, sagging, dying bloom. I should think young Chad must feel the same. Not that you're not still lovely. You are most certainly still lovely to me. Of course I'm so much older though, aren't I? So it really is relative, isn't it? There's always someone older, always someone younger . . . especially in the Grand Caymans of course.

"Those girls in the bikinis, they don't need white skirts with slits that show off only the part that serves to lure a man. They can show it all, eh? The whol-l-le thing. Because it's all young. Every delicious inch of moist, firm flesh . . . and tan . . . what does a young person worry about skin cancer or blotches, eh? They have all the luck, don't they? So unfair. So cruel."

Nora breathed out hard. She could hear her own breath almost snort out her nostrils. It was a sound she remembered her grandmother made.

"So you're saying," she said, trying to focus on him, "that Chaddy is going to dump me for some nubile nymphette?"

"With perky little tits," said Jack cheerfully. "Yes, of course that's what I'm saying."

"So what? At least I'll be rid of you. And if I lack for company, trust me, I can get it."

"Oh yes, of course," Jack said. He took her hand to his lips and kissed it. "Je vous en prie. I never meant to suggest that you didn't still have a dance or two left in you. Far from it. Quite the contrary. I am, after all, your most ardent admirer, really, Lovey, you know I think you're chust a knockout. Honest I do. No, no. In fact it's because you do hold all the cards in your relationship with Chad that I'm concerned for you. Who but you will know that he's murdered me? You see? And I'll be completely honest with you, Lovey, I work on that.

I play, on that with our Chad. It's my constant tune in fact, and of course he's so pliable, so subject to suggestion as we both know only too well. I tell him, 'Chad, Nora is going to dump you before you dump her.' I tell him how smart you are. Unlike me, he doesn't admire you for your mind. In fact I think he actually hates the fact that both of you know that he is so much duller than you. I see real resentment, which I do my utmost to encourage. I don't know if he will have confided this in you yet or not but I have in fact suggested to him that he and I form an alliance and that the two of us— after having faked my death of course—that the two of us then kill you. I think he's taken quite a shine to the idea. He doesn't trust you anymore, Lovey. He's afraid of you."

She knew that everything that Jack said had been true. She could no longer control him, arouse him, dangle him, and snap him back as once she had so easily been able to do. And he was frightened of her. And he didn't trust her. She knew that Jack would be talking to him just exactly the way he was talking to her now and that everything he said was true.

"You know I hide nothing from you, Lovey," he said. "You probably think I am duplicitous, a liar, but honestly, Lovey, I think I'm the most constant of life's companions. I don't lie to you. I never lie to you. I'm not like some Rotary Club person with their secret desires and secret envies, their secret fetishes that they have to go to some disease-infected bargain basement prostitute to fulfill. If I want you to probe some part of your body with a foreign object, I tell you. If I want you to do the same for me, I tell you, don't I? I don't run around with my dirty little secrets. I share them. I think, truly I do, that I'm the most honest of fellows. If I think you should have a lover, I tell you. If I think we can make some money out of the fact that you have a lover, I tell you that. I say, take the stupid lover. I know he doesn't mean anything to you. I know that you really have a pure heart and that he's little more than a vibrator, so I say, Come on Lovey, let's both use the vibrator boy toy. Let's pin my murder on him, and you and I will split the money. And I give you the ultimate gift of love, I even offer to set you free, though I swear to God, I love you. I do. I know you don't believe me, but I love you, Nora. I always have . . . always."

He was kneeling beside her and his face reflected itself in the mirror top, which held Nora's image as well. There were four of them there. Two Noras, two Jacks. He was crying. There were real tears. They welled up in his eyes and splashed his crying reflection, which was crying too.

"I love you because you and I are exactly the same. The world judges us harshly. But we don't judge each other. I don't judge you, Nora. Not even when I know that you and the lover I sent you to are plotting to kill me. I know . . . and I still don't judge you."

He stroked her hair gently and she closed her

eyes. She was so tired. She wanted to be a little girl, not again, but for the first time. She wanted finally to be a child and to rest safe and warm in someone's loving and protective embrace.

"Shhhhh, baby," Jack said, stroking her hair like a child, "Shhhhh little pussy, little innocent kitten. So when I know you are going to kill me, what should I do? Hmmm? In my place, Nora, what would you do?"

"Commit suicide," she said drily, but she did not tell him to take his hand off her hair or to stop stroking her like a little cat. It felt good.

"Ah well," he said, petting her, in his soothing old voice, "And don't think I haven't thought of it sometimes, my darling. Sometimes I've gone to sleep and prayed to never wake up. I'm so tired, Lovey, so tired of being Jack Wolfe. I want only sometimes to sleep, like a baby, and to be with you. But then I know you're going to kill me. You've got the very boy I sent you to. The very one that I wanted the two of us to use to buy our freedom, even if it meant freedom from each other. And I know now you plan to use that virile and powerful young fellow to murder me with my own plan no less. So what can I do to defend myself? Let me count the ways," he said as if reciting "How Do I Love Thee?"

"First," Jack said, taking hold of his own index finger, "I could kill you first. But I swear to you, Nora, that I love you, always have. I would sooner cut off, well, I won't lie.

"I wouldn't cut off my finger when you asked me to, but that's only because you know how I am about pain that has no sexual connotation. But the point is, as I think you understand, I'd much rather not kill you. You, my love, are the one that I want to screw my brains out with on some tropical island. You and I seducing natives of every sex, indulging every desire, and never judging each other. To me that is the meaning of love.

"Then, of course," said Jack, holding his middle finger, "I could kill Chad right now. But that would only call attention to ourselves and then of course who would we frame for my murder, which is of course the point of the whole thing; Then I'd be left with no one to frame but you. Out of the question, or only as a last resort, of course."

"Of course," she said. She felt warm and sleepy like a child fighting to stay awake to hear the end of a bedtime story but wanting so very much to curl up in a blankey and drift off like Winkin', Blinkin', and Nod.

"But there is a third way out of my dilemma. That you finally once and for all believe my sincerity. I'm a filthy degenerate, I don't hide that. I never have. It's the only thing I enjoy. But I don't lie to you, Nora. Ask yourself, isn't that true?"

In the most perverse sense of it all, it was true.

"So, here is the way. We plot my death on a boat with a bomb. But leave me a way out. One that Chad won't know about and the two of us will kill him, make it look like he died murdering me, didn't get far enough away from the explosion or something. We'll find the way, if we put our two good minds together I know we will, and we'll still get the money. I've worked out a way. Please say you will at least consider this, Lovey, because if you don't then I'll have no choice."

"No choice but to do what?" Nora asked like a child answering a parent reading a story who had said, "And *then* do you know what happened?"

"Why," Jack said, his eyes growing wide and innocent. "I'll have no choice but to help Chad kill you, of course. I don't lie, Lovey. You can't accuse me of lying. I tell you everything."

She knew that too was true.

"Just say you'll consider it, Lovey. That's all."

Like a princess forced to pledge her troth to an ogre in a fairy tale, Nora Wolfe said, "I will."

"That's all I ask, baby," Jack said tenderly, and she fell asleep.

Twelve

The whole island it seemed watched the three of them, Jack, Nora, and Chad, waiting to see what would happen, knowing surely that something would, smelling blood as surely as a shark smells it, except this time the blood had yet to be let. They simply knew it was coming.

Perhaps it was boredom. Since the hurricane there was little to do but watch and wait and drink or smoke. There was cleanup to be done, but the locals were pressured out. They had lived through a hurricane and now it was like "Whatevahs, ey bra?" An island lethargy had set in like mold. It spread over everything, sapping strength, draining interest. The phones were working again but a lot of places were still without electricity and a lot of the locals liked it that way. It was pau hanna every day. Kick back, slack key, shaved ice and brewskis and what? Talk story. That's what. Siddown, bruddah, talk story.

So the story was talked from Wailea up past Napili Point. People seen them, bruddah. Dat Haole lady, she used to be so fine, onolicious. Now she looked pale like a shark belly. The local girls would chime in about Chad, no good fun no more, jes smoke alla time. He looks green, ass why? 'Cause he smoke da kine alla time, ey?

It was as if the island had returned to earlier times before Captain Cook came looking for breadfruit to transplant to the Indies as a cheap source of food for British slaves. The island was verdant, and it seemed eager to devour once again all that the white and yellows had built on lands that were kapu to all but royals who fucked their own sisters and split each other's heads with war clubs. These people understood Jack and Nora and Chad. More than that. They appreciated them. For Haoles they were so Hawaiian. There were legends filled with this stuff. Songs and dances and rhythms beat on drums and bamboo, rolled on hips and belly flesh, songs of doomed princesses and babies ripped from wombs, angry sorcerers plotting murder and fecund warrior queens, cliffs that spat young lovers onto rocks below and gaping holes in mountains filled with hot pink bubbling, swallowing virgins, melting them, and gulping whole their tender limbs. Goddesses lived

in mountains full of witches' brew demanding trib-
ute, appeasement in blood lest their wrath bubble
over, burn with fiery licks down the mountains like
a devil licking virgin's thighs, tongues of flame and
torment, horny goddesses, jealous, unforgiving,
demanding blood. These people watched Jack and
Nora and Chad. The Polynesians understood
them.

The Chinese bet on them.

"Keep out of it," Joan Chan told me.

It was raining and the two of us sat in what
was left of a soon-to-be-closed bar called Lani's. I
watched Nora Wolfe cross Front Street, slip, and
stagger and try to make it look like it was the wet
pavement and not the vodka that made her trip so
awkwardly, so painfully clumsily down the street.

"Stay out of what?" I asked.

Joan didn't even dignify that one. She just said,
"I know more about this than you do. Stay out of
it. Let nature take its course. You can't make an arrest before the crime. It's not against the law to
think about murder, you know?"

I looked at her and in retrospect I imagine I
wore an expression of some pain or other.

"Someone's got to die," she said.

We used to talk about that when I was in the
army. There was an expression. The blood tax.
Someone's got to pay it. Sometimes we wouldn't
even look at each other because we knew someone, some one of us, was going to pay the blood
tax. It was just a question of who and when.

So too on the island now, the locals knew it. There was a passion tax and one of them or two or all three would pay in blood.

They talked it in the bars and in their back-yards. They barbecued in the drizzle, roasted pigs and skinned raw fish, gorged mouths with greasy fingers and talked about the three Haoles; the old one with the young wife who was fucking the boy; one was snorting, one was smoking, one was drinking.

There was money, too. The combinations were endless and the Chinese played them all, gave odds, and jiggled the line. Nora and Chad would kill Jack. Jack and Nora would kill Chad, Chad and Jack would do Nora, Nora would be killed killing Jack, Chad would be killed doing Nora. The three of them would die, the men would die, the woman, the boy, the man. Eyes watched them always, slant eyes, slit eyes, almond and round, yellow people, brown people, golden girls and boys and toothless hairy-cheeked hags, fat men with toothpicks, opium smokers and betel nut chewers, Madame DeFarge gone native sitting beneath a coconut tree instead of a gallows weaving grass hats instead of hair, taking odds, talking story, about murder.

"Stay out of it," Joan Chan said. "I know more about this than you do."

"I hate that kind of Third World mysterious racial shit, Joan," I said. "If you know something, say it. If you don't shut the fuck up."

"Stay out of it," she said.

* * *

And all the while Jack Wolfe played them both.

He played the Chad tune.

He told him, Watch out. Time's running short. You have one and only one chance to survive the spider. You know, the black widow who screws her prey into a coma and then spins him in her silk, wraps him in the silky threads she spews out from between her legs, holds him there in silky bondage, sticky ropes that slip around so quickly while his eyes glaze over, spent in lust, lost in a million spider orgasms until all he can do is lie there against the web and say, "What's that, dear, that sticky stuff? What is that? Dear . . . dear?" Charlotte does her shit and envelopes him in nature's own Saran Wrap until the sting, the numbing sting like the executioner's first shot, the tranquilizer before the lethal injection that holds him there in limbo till she's hungry enough to eat. You know that expression? You look good enough to eat? That's how Nora feels. Remember that. Think of it. As soon as you've served your purpose, you're dead. You believe that, don't you?

Chad didn't know what he believed anymore.

Your only salvation lies with me, Jack would tell him. If you don't believe me, watch Nora. Watch the way she acts. You'll see. You'll see, mein kindt.

So Chad watched Nora.

And while Chad watched Nora, Jack played her song as well.

I have the boy convinced you're going to kill him, he would tell her. He believes me like his long lost poppa, his estranged deadbeat daddy who's finally come for his birthday party and will disappoint him no more. The answer to his secret prayer. He knows you're going to kill him and he knows too, that the only way he can survive is to trust me and help me kill you.

"I've done it all for you, Lovey," Jack told her. "I've turned your lover against you in order to save you. Because now you know that you have to throw in with me and kill Chad, otherwise he and I will kill you. I'm telling you all this so you can save yourself, which is all I ever wanted. I was the one, if you recall, who suggested we fake my death and frame the boy in the first place. You, Lovey, were the one who changed the rules. I just adapted to them like a jujitsu artist and used your own momentum against you. Now the only way you can save yourself is by betraying our Chad. But what is he anyway? He's a dildo, batteries not included. He's a cucumber. He was made to be sliced."

And the plan?

The problem was of course that Jack had named both Nora and Jean as the beneficiaries on his insurance.

He had told Chad, "You will be Jean."

He had told Chad, "You will be Jean and with Nora dead you will inherit everything."

Thus it was only natural that he was now

telling Nora, that with Jean dead she would do the same.

But how could Jean be dead if Jean was Chad and they needed Chad alive long enough to frame him for Jack's murder and *then* kill him, or at least make it look as if he had died in the same explosion that would have taken Jack's life?

"The answer, my dear," Jack said, "is Nigeria."

Nigeria, you will recall, was Jack's fabled land of possibilities, where the right amount of money could buy anything, everything.

"Listen, Lovey," he said. "I think you'll really get a kick out of this. I'm going to have Chad take his pictures, or I'll take the pictures of him, you know. These will be pictures that he is going to think are for his passport. I'll get his fingerprints for the bureaucracy stuff, yeah? But I'm not chust going to get a passport for him, I'm going to get a death certificate too. And the date of death of poor Jean will be before my own untimely end. In that way, my son and heir will have died before me and so all the money will be paid to my grieving widow . . . to you, Lovey, just like we planned. And it won't even be that big of a lie because of course we're going to kill Chad anyway. Once I have the documents I'll make sure they're forwarded to a friend of mine, a friend whom I trust implicitly. If, after my supposed murder I am still alive, he will receive a signal from me. Upon receiving that signal, he will forward the documents attesting to poor Jean's death to the bank in Liechtenstein. The banker, Monsieur Tessler, receiving absolute proof that Jean's death preceded mine will have no choice but to inform the insurance company that the sole living beneficiary is you, Lovey."

Nora's head was swimming. It was like watching a three-card monte dealer on mescaline.

Jack's smile changed to a stern look, the look of a sadistic parent warning his victim of tortures yet to come for infractions of the house rules.

"On the other hand, if you are foolish enough to turn aside my almost selflessly generous offer, and if you side with that callow boy against your sweet Jack, your only true soul mate in life, then not only will the angels weep for you, but that same trusted friend will forward to our flatfoot, Detective Kahana, copies of the infamous Dear Jean letters in which I confide to my child that my young wife and her much younger lover are, I fear, conspiring to kill me. And don't you think," Jack said, "that I already have certain pieces of physical evidence, fingerprints on certain objets de murder, shall we say, ready to be revealed at the proper time? Don't you think that I've taken that precaution?"

Nora was sure that he had.

"If you don't believe that the danger is very real, watch our Chad," he told her. "Watch how he acts. You'll see, little pussy. You'll see, kitten. Sweet Jack is the only one you can trust."

So, despite herself Nora watched Chad.

And Chad watched Nora.

The whole island watched the three of them.

Joan Chan watched me and said, "Stay out of it."

Thirteen

On the day that Nora Wolfe found out that her husband Jack did not intend to kill her lover Chad after all, that he had perhaps never, in fact, intended to kill him but had always indeed, from the very beginning intended to kill *her*, it broke her heart.

It was physical.

She could feel it.

It was as if something living had cracked inside her chest, the dull ache, the breathing that came now with difficulty, that struggled to send impulses to muscles to pull the rib cage, expand lungs, force in the air and then out again like an old squeeze box wheezing out a tune, like a Mozart requiem, like a consumptive dying, like a broken heart, she thought, exactly like a broken heart.

It was an aside, a moment of parenthetical epiphany—ah yes, so that's why they call it a broken heart—that eased the pain not a bit, that helped the old, slow alcoholic fluid in the lungs breathing not at all. It was simply a name for the disease, not a cure, not even a balm.

So this is a broken heart.

This is all those smoky songs, this is the thing that no one ever tells you. This is the price for loving those unworthy of love, for pearls of hope and trust cast before swine, this is the blues.

She was a bright woman and the irony was not lost on her, but to her dull surprise a sense of irony did not help a broken heart either. For she had believed, and had not realized until now. How much she counted on that belief, how much of a cornerstone it was to the world she had built, brick by heavy, painful brick, that in his own tortured, degenerate, perverted and profane way, that Jack Wolfe, her husband Jack, loved her.

She had thought that after all had been said and done, that Jack with his degenerate lies had never lied to *her,* that the truth of drugs and illicit sex with men and women, children and objects inserted and expelled, meant that in hiding nothing, masking no desire no matter how base, he had been, in what he would call his own sweet, sick way, true to her in his fashion,

true to her in his way, the most constant, in
fact, of lovers, who judged her not, and accepted
whatever judgment she cared to pass upon him
and yet still wear the gold band, the golden
shackle, the sign of the willing slave upon his
finger, the wedding ring that said, I, who am so
truly not of this society, nor of these rules nor
bourgeois hypocracies you call morals, I, who
believe in nothing and no one, ever, believe
nonetheless, in you. I, despite the fact that you
despise me, loathe me, lie to me, plot to murder
me with the lover to whose bed I sent you, I
nonetheless love, in this world of nothing I can't
betray . . . you.

Inexplicably, you.

A miracle, you.

I, who lie about everything, admit it, and
therefore lie about nothing, lie not about this single truth, for God (in whom I don't believe, only
fear) only knows what reason, love, if you too are
sick enough to name this sickness love, then I . . .
love you.

She had even imagined herself, played out the
scene in her mind in fact, after he was dead, after
she and her boy toy had killed him, she would,
paying for it with the money for which she had
murdered him, raise a glass of some rum punch or
other, in some exotic bar whose lighting made her
look ten years younger, raise a glass to him, look
into her murdering accomplice's eyes and say,

"But you don't understand, underneath it all, he loved me."

It was the one thing that comforted her.

And she would need comfort after all. She would be his widow.

The Widow Wolfe, whose late husband, despite his murder, died knowing she had outsmarted him, smiling perhaps, loving, more than forgiving, and proud.

It was a lie.

It was a lie, she thought, oh God, a lie. She had never felt so betrayed. She had never felt so bereft, so alone, so lonely and hopeless as a two A.M. busstop diner.

He didn't love her after all.

The betrayal turned to hurt.

The hurt turned to anger.

The anger to hatred.

The hatred so powerful, she could kill him, which was of course what she had intended to do anyway, but now would do without remorse or any romantic notions.

There would be no raised glass in some exotic bar.

No tear that glimmered for an instant as she silently toasted the man she'd killed who loved her after all, whose love only she could understand, because it was, after all, for her.

No. The illusions were gone.

From here on out, this was business.

*   *   *

She had known the minute Chad had told her.

She had known the minute Chad had told her how he intended to kill her.

She had known the minute Chad had told her how he, Jack, had intended to kill her because he, Jack, had not told her this was the way he intended to kill Chad.

Heretofore there had been a delicious symmetry. Whatever Jack told Nora, he told Chad that he had told Nora. Then he would tell Chad something new and tell Nora he had told Chad that same new something.

But this time she was not included.

This time Jack and Chad had a secret.

It was how they would kill Nora.

It was so like Jack.

He didn't even trust the sharks.

He had explained to Chad or rather posed his explanation first in the guise of a question.

"What if the sharks don't eat everything?" he'd said.

"What do you mean?" Chad had characteristically asked.

"I mean," said Jack, "what if they're full, what if they ate something that didn't agree with them and their stomachs are queasy, what if their legendary voracious appetites prove to be just that: a legend. What if they're trying to cut down on meat intake or are celebrating Shark Ramadan, Lent, or Yom Kippur, what then?"

Chad didn't get it.

"What if they don't finish all the peas on their plate? What if they don't eat everything, you dolt?" Jack finally asked. "What if we cave in her skull with a ball peen hammer and the sharks eat everything but the skull and some smart, enterprising Oriental coroner looks at the skull and says, 'Shark not kill this woman unless shark own a set of hand tools complete with ball peen hammer.' "

"What if we shoot the bitch," Jack said, growing testy. "Let's say we shoot the bitch, okay? Let's say just for the sake of argument that we were stupid enough to shoot Nora before we blow her up, all right? Then let's say that the explosion sends her sky high and we are unlucky enough to get a diarrhetic herd of sharks and they don't eat all the Nora on their plates. And let's say Glen Yamamoto or whatever Coroner Glen's last name may prove to be, examines the skull and says, 'Shark not kill lady unless Shark knows how to fire a thirty-eight automatic.' We're fucked then, aren't we, Chad? Our whole plan is kaput because we didn't foresee a shark with a wanting appetite. Well I say, let's foresee it, shall we?"

So he suggested Seconal.

Well everyone knew she had a habit, popped pills, couldn't hold her liquor, was a drunk, a lush, something pathetic really, stumbling down the street like that, so who would question it? Say the explosion didn't rip her apart. Say the sharks didn't finish the meal. Say Glen got enough of something to autopsy, to run through their horrible snooping machines that said whose blood was whose and what they'd drunk, or eaten, snorted or smoked. What would they find?

Seconal?

Surprise, surprise!

The drug addict had drugs.

The drunkard's been drinking.

Not poisoned, mind you. No foul play. Just addiction and abuse.

She was with her husband. They'd been drinking, fucking, fighting, ingesting, whatever it was that everyone knew they did. It would in fact help with the story of the explosion. Well they were both so stoned, you know? Maybe it wasn't even murder. Just an accident. Just the ultimate outcome. Who was the actor, the movie star drunk who slipped and hit his head and died not of drink or trauma, but loss of blood, who sat there with the towel around his head on the kitchen floor, too drunk to do anything but bleed?

"Seconal," Jack told Chad.

Injectable Seconal. One quick shot.

Good night. *Kaboom.* Good night.

*   *   *

"That's probably what he told you," Chad said.

"What?" she'd asked, just beginning to feel the shock as her head reeled with the thought that Jack had lied and didn't love her after all.

"That's probably the way he told you, that's how the two of you should kill me," Chad said.

"Oh," said Nora. "Yes. yes, that's what he said. Seconal. Kill Chad with Seconal."

"That's what I figured," Chad said, happy that he had finally caught on to how the grown-ups played the game.

As for her, Nora was too ashamed to admit to her lover that her husband favored him over her, trusted him over her, perhaps loved him, who knows, Jack was certainly capable of that, more than her.

So jealousy fed it as well. Jealousy that maybe her husband found her sleek-skinned seal boy sexier than her and her aging tits.

And there was more than jealousy.

There was fear. Fear that if Chad knew . . . knew that Jack had trusted him and not Nora, that perhaps Chad would reciprocate. Perhaps he could be flattered, his young head turned, his boyish fancy charmed by Jack, sweet Jack, the lying, soon-to-be-oh-so-very-dead toad of a Jack, that Jack who could charm anyone with his faithless love.

How she hated him.

How fixed she was now, how focused so singly upon his death. It was all she wanted. All that mattered, and despite her protestations, it was not business now.

It was personal.

And of course that's just what Jack was counting on.

Fourteen

Nora knew that the secret to killing her husband and getting away with it lay in finding the trusted friend. He was Jack's ace in the hole, the one who would wait for the signal, who would forward to the police, to me in fact, incriminating evidence, puzzle pieces that when placed jagged edge to edge would form a picture of murder. Without the trusted friend, Jack was dead. Well, truth be told, she had made up her mind Jack was dead one way or the other, but without the trusted friend she would get away with it. She and Chad would have the money and each other until money or interest in each other wore out.

Chad had told her of the plan, the plan to use Seconal and then blow her up.

She had told Chad that that was exactly what Jack was planning for him as well. Yes, she said, Exactly the same words, Seconal and then blow him up.

So, that's what they would do to Jack, with his own Seconal, the same injectable barbiturate he had procured from his Chinese medicine man. Always it was the Chinese! That's where he got the tooth, or rather who pulled it. Some Chinaman.

And that's when she knew.

The trusted friend was an Oriental.

Had to be.

No question about it.

She began making a list of other things the trusted friend had to be. It was a list of deductive reasoning based on the one subject in which she believed she had earned a doctorate, Jack Wolfe.

First, he was Chinese.

This gave them a secret language in which to communicate, a veil between them and the white world.

Next, more than likely he would be from Shanghai and he would be from the old days, from the days of Jack's youth, from his drug running days in Vietnam and Vientiane, from the days with Sonny Trafficante, working out of the U.S. residence in Phnom Penh, from the time of living dangerously, Indochine, Shanghai, the remnants of the Green Gang and men who knew Big Eared Tu and ran Chiang Kai-shek.

He would be someone on whom Jack had

something. That was a given. Just like Nora, Jack let no one in his life on whom he didn't have leverage. Jack had something on everybody. If he didn't, you weren't his friend.

It would be someone close. She doubted that the trusted friend would have been someone who lived here in Maui all along. It was an island after all. People knew everything. But it would be someone whom he had moved closer since they had been plotting his death. He would want that, want him close at hand. The trusted friend was here then, on the island, with them, watching, waiting for his cue to make his entrance.

Finally, if Jack was paying him and had been paying him for all these years a retainer of some sort, the money would be modest but meaningful. Two thousand a month, say. No less than fifteen hundred or so, no more than three thousand. She doubted it would be three thousand.

Finally, Jack would have found a way to deduct it.

He would not have paid all this money all this time without being able to claim it somehow as a write-off.

That's how she would find him.

The money would lead her to the trusted friend.

Their taxes, corporate and personal, were filed jointly. She was an officer in all sixteen of his companies. She had the returns.

She poured over them day and night, grew to

know them more intimately than any lover's body. The numbers were her allies, secret informers pointing her this way, then that. They were bread-crumbs in an evil forest that led to light, that led her to the only other person who might have to die, the trusted friend.

His name was Wang.

He was old.

He was from Shanghai, probably in the country illegally.

He had lived in Maui before she'd married Jack, then moved to the big island, then to Eva side Honolulu, then up to Waienai, wherever Jack's dealings needed someone he could trust.

He had moved back to Maui, to a shack outside Lahaina, inland up past the old plantations.

He was listed as a florist now, had been listed as a gardener, house cleaner, auto repairman, pool man, house man, driver, caretaker, gatekeeper, watchman, and cook. But the money was always the same, adjusted every so often for inflation, it ran to twenty-two hundred fifty a month now.

The plan was simple. Since Wang was waiting for a signal, Wang would have to be dealt with at exactly the same time that Jack was being dealt with. Chad would kill Jack, drug him first with the Seconal, then set the timer on the boat that would blow it to bits and Jack along with it, bludgeon him into bite-sized pieces for the sharks who slept in the seven caves until the smell of blood would wake them, call them up from their depths with the siren song of death.

Wang would either give her the documents she needed or she would kill him, and then frame Chad for it, of course. That was the fallback position if things got messy.

Chad did it.

She had already plotted it out, planted the evidence, pocketed an ashtray with his prints on it to plant in the house of Wang, the trusted friend.

She felt a real sense of accomplishment, for the first time in her life perhaps.

This was hers.

She had conceived it, planned it, improvised against adversity, covered all the angles, figured the percentages and the odds, planned for rainy days, and made her hay in the sunshine. She had been as diligent as a school girl lusting after honors. She had campaigned for this.

It was a clean feeling, like when your floors were spotless, your linens clean, your shelves freshly lined with paper.

It was a new house, pristine underwear, a fresh start.

It was all that Easter promised, resurrection and new birth.

It was the first spring day of her life.

She was going to kill her husband and get away with it.

Fifteen

What happened on May 15th is largely a matter of conjecture based on the little physical evidence that was left and the testimony of the only participant to be left alive. Thus, its reliability is suspect at best, and certain facets, in fact, in retrospect according to what is now known, or at least suspected, proved to be completely wrong.

But this, for what it's worth, is what wound up in the legal record.

At shortly past seven-thirty A.M. on a Sunday, the fifteenth of May, an explosion was heard from Lahaina to Wailea.

The fireball was visible up to Kaanapali.

The explosion in question was aboard the

powerboat *Circe,* a beautiful old wooden-hulled pleasure craft owned by Jack and Nora Wolfe.

Later DNA testing of a tooth and blood splatters on pieces of decking which were ultimately recovered indicated that at least one of the victims was in fact Jack Wolfe. Some of his clothing was recovered. But his body was never found. Officials believed it was eaten by sharks.

The other victim is believed to have been an unemployed former bartender and local surfer by the name of Chad Clinton Sellers, aged twenty-three, who was evidently having an affair with the deceased's widow, Nora Wolfe. Remains of his body were found. They had been eaten by sharks but a tibia was found almost intact, and part of a femur as well, and with DNA testing, those bones were positively identified as having come from the deceased's wife's much younger lover.

Nora Wolfe was arrested at seven-forty A.M., May 15th, at the home of one Wang En Lai, also known as Ernie Wang, a seventy-two-year-old part-time cook, driver, and occasional gardener. Video-tape taken by the police from a hidden camera was presented at her trial and shows her threatening to kill Mr. Wang unless he produced various documents which Mrs. Wolfe evidently believed would prove her undoing should they fall into the hands of the authorities.

The arrest was made by Det. Denil Kahana and Det. Sgt. Joan Chan, who it turns out was also the granddaughter of Wang en Lai, an undocumented alien originally from Shanghai.

Mrs. Wolfe was sentenced to life in prison without the possibility of parole.

Mr. Wang was ordered deported to Taiwan since he was the holder of a valid passport for that embattled island nation.

Det. Sgt. Chan resigned from the department. The locals attributed her resignation to an Oriental face-saving gesture brought on by the disgrace of her grandfather's association with a known racketeer and his subsequent deportation.

Det. Sgt. Chan escorted her grandfather back to Taipei.

So much for the legal record.

Within two weeks of Wang's supposed deportation and Joan Chan's disgrace, a respected banker by the name of Tessler in the fairy-tale principality of Liechtenstein, looked up from the papers spread before him, adjusted his spectacles on his nose, and said, "Well, my dear Jean, at last we meet. I only wish it had been under pleasanter circumstances."

Joan Chan smiled.

Sixteen

According to interviews I personally con-
ducted with Banker Tessler some three
months after the fact at the behest of the insurance
company, Jean Wolfe had presented documentation that showed her to be a female Vietnamese
who had been orphaned and adopted by one Jack
Wolfe in Vietnam, raised and educated by private
tutors in Switzerland, and was now a citizen and
resident of Nigeria, where she owned and operated
a thriving import/export business. In addition to
the normal documentation, she produced letters
from her late father Jack that spoke of his concern
that his young wife and her much younger lover
were plotting to kill him.

When I showed Banker Tessler the Maui

County I.D. photo of Joan Chan, he positively identified it as being Jean Wolfe, Jack Wolfe's only living heir.

Moreover, it turns out that Banker Tessler was so taken with Ms. Wolfe's exotic good looks that his gaze lingered upon her until she crossed out of the bank and, within view of his window, into the arms of an elderly Oriental gentleman whom I can only assume was Grandpa Wang.

Most interesting of all, there appears to have been a third individual. There is a very grainy surveillance camera photo of him. He was standing in the bank, passing the time enquiring about accounts and interest rates on various certificates of deposit. Then shortly after Jean's departure, he left. Banker Tessler is prepared to swear under oath that this individual, who appeared to be still powerful-looking in his late fifties or early sixties, joined Jean Wolfe and the elderly Oriental gentleman outside the bank, and that after a romantic embrace with Ms. Wolfe, the three of them got into a Mercedes taxi cab and sped off.

Nora had known it all along.

"He's alive," she had hissed, almost from the beginning. Somehow, she wasn't sure of the particulars, Jack was alive, not only alive but enjoying the fruits of his labors.

It was only after Joan Chan resigned that she screamed, "The Chink!" She rambled in a kind of delirium about the various possibilities. Jack was the one who had somehow helped out Joan's grandfather, or Jack was connected to the grandfather from the old days in Shanghai, perhaps having saved his life and receiving in return, Wang's first granddaughter, Joan. He had seduced her, he had won her, he had owned her, willed her, deeded her, had bought her, or received her as collateral. Whatever it was, it was insignificant in comparison with the one fact which Nora knew beyond any doubt . . . he *owns* her. Together they had engineered poor Chad's death, or perhaps Chad was in on it with them, still alive, shtupping Jack or Chan or Wang for all she knew, until Nora remembered the tibia, or fibia, or whatever the hell bones of Chad's they'd found.

No. Poor, stupid, sleek-skinned Chad was dead.

But Jack was alive.

That was the point.

He was alive and in cahoots with Chan and Wang and together they had pulled it off, framed Nora, killed Chad, and gotten the money and were now, even now, raising a glass in the Bahamas to poor Nora, who made it all possible.

Then we heard about the plane crash.

It seems a plane en route from Liechtenstein to Zurich, connecting with various flights for the Seychelles Islands, had crashed. The problem was a faulty air speed indicator and pilot error.

All aboard perished.

Listed as passengers were one Jean Wolfe of Nigeria, Wang en Lai of Taiwan, and another passenger traveling on a Nigerian passport by the name of Yaakov Ze'ev. Yaakov Ze'ev is Hebrew for Jack Wolfe.

Go figure.

The minute Nora began babbling they called me. She had been screaming my name.

She told me everything. From the beginning.

I contacted the insurance company.

The insurance company was only too happy to have a possible explanation that would allow them to recoup their losses, so after I quit the department they hired me.

Nora was only too happy to have someone out there trying to prove that Jack was alive, at least, at the time that the insurance money was paid out by Banker Tessler in Liechtenstein. Because if he had been alive in Liechtenstein, then he wasn't dead in Maui.

If he wasn't dead in Maui, Nora wasn't guilty of having killed him.

If she wasn't guilty of having killed him, she would not have to be in state prison for life without possibility of parole. The insurance company paid for the flight to Liechtenstein and my expenses tracking down Jack and Joan and Wang prior to their ill-fated takeoff. Unfortunately, the state of Hawaii has not bought it yet.

We're up on appeal.

On the day that Nora found out about the plane crash she shouted out loud, "Son of a bitch! There is a God!"

It was the final sense of irony that appealed to

her and confirmed for her the existence of an omniscient deity with a warped sense of humor.

She assumed he was Jewish.

That's when she decided to convert.

I had known numerous convicts who had been born again in prison.

They usually signed onto the program in order to make parole.

I explained to Nora that being Jewish would get her no points with a Hawaiian parole board, but it seemed not to matter.

"God's a Jew," she'd said, "and I'm with him."

I found a rabbi from Chabad of Lahaina.

He had come to do the Passover Seder at the Sheraton and had been ordered by the Rebbe himself, when the latter was, it appears, delusional, to stay in Lahaina and save the Jews thereof from apostasy.

He agreed, after countless hours of Talmudic debate to undertake the conversion of Nora Wolfe.

We celebrate Shabbat together now.

Nora, Chabad of Lahaina, me, and Schvester Rochelle, Sister Rachel, formerly chaplain of Honolulu P.D.

After Schvester retired from the chaplaincy, she sank into a deep melancholia which so concerned the Monsignor of Honolulu that an APB was put out to find a purpose for Schvester's life without the cops.

I suggested Nora Wolfe.

I told one and all who would listen that the one

thing Sister Rachel never had and wanted above all else was a daughter.

Well the one thing that Nora wanted more than anything else was a mother figure . . . voila! They were made for each other.

Sister Rachel didn't even care that Nora was going to convert to Judaism. She took her under her wing like a mother duck.

So every Friday, Nora Wolfe and I joined Chabad of Lahaina and Schvester Rochelle the Blue Nun, for Shabbas.

The Major keeps telling me that it is only because Nora hopes to use me to find that Jack was alive in Liechtenstein and thereby hopes to prove she wasn't guilty of having murdered him in Lahaina, that she is with me.

That may or may not be true.

I only know that the talks we have had since her incarceration have been the most honest I have ever had with any woman, ever. There is no deceit of any kind. There is no need for it.

She tells me about plotting to kill her husband and I tell her how much I loved her, always.

The Major says that if the state approves conjugal visits I will have the perfect woman: horny, appreciative, and locked up, so you know where you can find her.

The truth is, for Nora and me, maybe it is perfect. Nora for the first time lives in an environment where they control every waking hour. If she